# Redeeming Grace

## A Story of Redemption

### By

### Bridget T. Crawford

## Thank you!!

Jesus, you continue to blow my mind! Thank you for this gift. Thank you for the gift of Your life! To my amazing husband, Tyrone Crawford. Thank you for always encouraging me, always having my back, always loving me like crazy. I can't be mediocre around you because you naturally bring out the best in me. I love you so much! Thanks for always encouraging me to utilize my gifts. Without you, I don't even know if this book would've ever gotten written! To my daughter Kyira, thank you for being so compassionate, don't ever let anyone corrupt that. Keep caring! To my son, Isaiah. Thank you for being so caring. You're going to be a great leader! I love y'all! To my mom, Mary Taylor, thank you for always supporting me. Thank you for all the movies growing up, they helped to cultivate my passion for the fiction genre and great plots. Love you! To my dad, thank you! You're so supportive and loving. Glad I can come to you with the wealth of knowledge you possess in that brain of yours. I love you! To all my siblings, Ericka, Crystal, Tony, Dale, Thomas, and Christle, I love y'all!!

# Chapter 1:

"Ma!!" Grace yelled down the stairs to her mother. "Can I wear your yellow sweater? Damien and I decided to go to the parade tonight." The Church of Second Chance's had been Tasha and her daughter Grace's home church since Grace was a toddler. They were having a parade that night to celebrate fifteen years of ministry in the city of Baltimore. Tasha was looking forward to attending with her daughter, but she sprained her ankle a few days earlier while exercising and was sentenced to the dreaded crutches for a few more weeks. She wasn't excited about that. She and Grace had a very close relationship, one that other mothers and daughters really admired, they loved finding attending events. She also hated wasting a good Friday night. Also, Tasha wasn't very fond of Damien, Grace's boyfriend of almost two months, he just did not rub her the right way. To Tasha, Damien seemed to have a lot going for himself, but it all just seemed a little too perfect. He presented himself as an outstanding young man who respected women, loved children, gave back, loved God, had a full ride scholarship to Howard University, helped elderly ladies across the street, kept at-risk-youth off the street, and had even started attending church with Grace and Tasha. He was in the process of visiting churches. Damien had expressed to them that the one he was attending on campus had just gotten a new pastor who just didn't sit right with Damien.

"Sure," Tasha responded reluctantly, as Grace came down the stairs to join her mother for dinner.

"Well, now I don't want to wear it anymore." Grace replied.

"Sorry, Grace Face, I just really wanted to go tonight, plus I don't trust that little boyfriend of yours."

"Ma, I am convinced that you have some sort of vendetta against Damien. Seriously, can you think of anything he's done that would cause you not to trust him?"

"I know. That's the problem, he's too nice, overly nice like he has something to hide. Plus he's a grown man. How-ever, it may just be my crazy mama-bear paranoia, I mean your dad was definitely the perfect man. I wonder if Mom thought this about Ernest, you know, that your dad was too nice, too perfect. He was definitely a true gentleman, that's for sure!" Although Tasha did not care for Damien, she wanted Grace to know that she was aware she was growing up and didn't want to push her away before she left for college next year.

"Ma, he's only three years older than me, actually two, since I'll be eighteen in two months, five days and three hours. Daddy was five years older than you, and y'all were married for fifteen years, love doesn't have an age requirement. 'And when love speaks, the voice of all the gods makes Heaven drowsy with the harmony.'"

"Girl, please. Here she goes quoting Shakespeare. First of all, don't forget Shakespeare also wrote Romeo and Juliet, and we all know what happened in that story, second of all, it's been less than two months, you better not love that boy. Third of all, you're trippin' with that birthday countdown."

Tasha and Grace were both literary enthusiasts and randomly quoted authors, both to each other and to their friends. People thought they were kind of strange for that since they didn't usually see African Americans quoting literary work, but that's what made their bond so unique, they were different in their own way and didn't care.

"Nah, you definitely don't have to worry about that yet, there's no love here, I don't think. It's way too early for all of that, but I do like him a lot," Grace blushingly replied.

Grace is a senior at Balentine High School in Baltimore, Maryland. An outstanding honor student who loves literature, art, music, volleyball, basketball, golf … in fact there aren't a lot of things that Grace didn't like. She did not confine herself to one activity, she wanted to be the person that enjoys life, and she views that as doing as many things as possible to avoid missing anything that may interest her even more. Tasha respects her daughter's enthusiasm and spunk, but she often gets on Grace's case about this because, although she wants Grace to be multitalented and unrestricted, she wants to make sure Grace understands the importance of being focused. As intelligent and talented as Grace is, she still has no idea what her focus will be in college, and that is just driving Tasha up the wall. Although Grace will be attending college with no financial obligation, she wants to make sure Grace takes full advantage of that. Ernest, Tasha's husband, and Grace's dad was in the Army but was killed in an IED attack while deployed to Iraq two years ago. Grace's dad was huge on education and wanted to make sure his daughter had the best opportunities, so he transferred his educational benefits a year before he was killed. The three of them had the best relationship a family could ask for, so his death took a severe toll on Grace and Tasha. They were emotionally, spiritually, and mentally depleted during that period. As a result of that, Grace and Tasha found themselves always at odds with each other, they couldn't seem to get along, but they were both just hurting, bitter and, to top it off, they realized they were furious at God.

It wasn't until a year ago that their relationship began to return to normal, and they were finally beginning to heal. They knew Ernest would not have wanted them to be at each other's throats, he would want them to move on and love on each other. Ernest loved Jesus immensely and always expressed the importance of dealing with things. He was not a sweep-things-under-the-rug kind of guy, he understood that if you didn't get to the root of an issue that things will continue to spiral out of control, and that is what Grace and Tasha had to do, get to the source of their bickering and fighting. They decided to go to some therapy sessions that their church was offering, and it was in those sessions that they realized they'd never adequately dealt with the pain of losing Ernest, it happened so suddenly, abruptly, and traumatically that they never gave themselves time to process it, so they took it out on each other. Once they admitted what was going on and allowed God to heal them, they were on their way to being individually restored and restoring their relationship. Now, their relationship is better than it's ever been. Ernest always called their daughter Grace Face, so during their therapy sessions, Tasha adopted her late husband's pet name and has been calling Grace that ever since. It allows them to keep a piece of Ernest in their everyday conversations.

After dinner, Grace asked her mother if she needed anything before Damien arrived to pick her up. Tasha assured her that she was fine and urged her daughter to have a great time and not to worry about her. "When you get off those crutches, we are going to Zumba class. Just be careful not to do anything beyond your age ability, that's how you ended up in those crutches in the first place," Grace says jokingly as Tasha gives her an annoyed look.

"Oh, you are a comedian tonight, don't make me hit you with one of these crutches, I will just tell the hospital that I accidentally stepped on you while you were asleep on the floor."

Looking unimpressed with her mother's attempt at a joke, Grace responded: "They will not believe you for two reasons, why would I be asleep on the floor, and how could you not see me on the floor?"

"It makes perfect sense. See, I wouldn't see you on the floor because it would be midnight, and all of the lights are off. You fell asleep watching TV and rolled off the couch unto the floor, and the TV auto shut off because of inactivity. So, it was pitch black in the living room. I went downstairs to get my cell phone charger out of the living room, not expecting someone to be lying on the floor, so I stepped right on your face with the crutch. You screamed, it startled me, and in response to the piercing shriek, I swung my crutch, this time making contact with your arm. That, my friend, is my story, and I'm sticking to it."

"So, for you to just sit here and concoct that psychotic story, I am convinced that you need to stop watching the ID channel and Lifetime, that's not an acceptable imagination for a sane person." Grace and Tasha burst into laughter, interrupted by the blaring sound of a car horn.

"Oh shoot, Damien's here, I need to go grab my phone." As Grace runs upstairs to grab her phone, Tasha peers out the window at the orange sports car parked outside of her house, she thinks to herself, *maybe Damien really is a great guy, my daughter seems infatuated with him, and she's a pretty bright girl, she'd be able to sense a creep, right? I guess I'll let her live a little.*

"Okay, I found it, but it's barely charged. Ugh." Grace shouts to her mom as she races down the stairs, heading for the door. As she begins to open the door, she pauses, realizing she hadn't properly said bye to her mother. "Sorry, Ma," Grace exclaimed, as she kissed her mother on the cheek. "I'll be back in a couple of hours; are you sure you don't need me to bring you anything from the store?"

"Sure, if you guys stop anywhere, you can grab some paper towels, and tell Damien I said hello."

"Huh, are you high? You want me to tell Damien that you said hello?"

Laughing, Tasha assured Grace, "No, I am not high, just thought I'd give the boy a chance unless he gives me a reason not to like him; it's only fair right?"

"Thanks, Ma, see, that's why I love you!" Grace runs out of the door to meet Damien in his Mustang as Tasha looks on with pride. Feeling so grateful that Grace is turning into a bright young woman, she couldn't ask God for a better daughter.

# Chapter 2

"Man, this church has done a lot for this city, I guess I can call myself blessed to be a part of it," Grace expressed to Damien as they peered into the crowd full of paradegoers.

"Why do you say you guess?"

"I don't know, maybe because I feel like I could do more to contribute to the outreaches they facilitate."

"But you do help with some, right?"

"Yep," replied Grace with a smile on her face.

"Then I wouldn't focus on the ones you didn't help with, or what you didn't do, pat yourself on the back for what you did contribute. If you go through life focusing on what you didn't do, or what you could have done, it takes away the shine from the great things you, in fact, did accomplish. Don't live with regrets Grace; it's exhausting."

"Woah, that was some profound wisdom you just spit right there! Howard must be shaping some fine, intelligent young men."

Damien smirks, then laughs. "That great thing you say is true, Grace, glad I met someone who appreciates my great wisdom, haha."

"You know, you're pretty unique Damien, I can honestly say I've never met anyone like you. I think you're definitely in your own world, which is a good thing. Hope you never change my mind about that." Grace says smirking. She looks over at Damien's dark brown face, waiting for him to respond to the compliment she'd just given him. Instead, she catches him staring into the crowd with a bothered look on his face. "Oh, guess I'm talking to myself, that's cool, I'm an only child I got used to it years ago," Grace exclaims with sarcasm.

"Sorry Grace, I did hear you, I was just processing what you said. Well, I hope I don't ever make you change your—"

"Damien! What's up, bro? This must be Grace, yo bro, she sure is beautiful."

Damien is interrupted by a very large, attractive young man who approaches them while they were sitting on the park bench. *"He's huge,"* Grace thinks, with a slight feeling of intimidation. *"I wonder if he's some kind of bouncer."*

"Yes, this is Grace. Grace, this is Leon, my roommate at Howard, a-k-a the ladies linebacker. Leon, this is my girl, Grace." Damien often told Grace stories about Leon, how he'd messed around with way too many women. Leon was a linebacker for Howard University and had quite the reputation for being a ladies man.

"Aye man don't call me that, you know I don't want that negative connotation attached to my name. Nice to meet you, Grace, I've heard a lot about you."

"Likewise, Leon," Grace responds, reluctantly. Grace did not know Leon, but from the stories she'd heard from Damien, she had a feeling that he wouldn't be her favorite person in the world. Grace's dad always told her to give people the benefit of the doubt and to treat people with respect, so in spite of what Damien told her about Leon, she wasn't going to treat him any differently, but she did have her guard up. In her eyes, a womanizer would go to any lengths to get the woman they wanted, even their roommate's girl. So, Grace kept an open eye for any signs that Leon was trying to flirt with her or disrespect Damien in front of her. Grace learned quite a bit from her dad. He was not the man to sugarcoat the important things in life, and he was well-rehearsed with these tactics and tricks because he was quite the ladies' man himself before meeting her mom and settling down. She feels fortunate to have gotten that knowledge from her dad before he passed away, and she feels confident that he would have approved of Damien. That was one of the reasons why she couldn't understand why her mother felt Damien was so sketchy. He had all of the qualities in a boyfriend that a mother would love for her daughter's boyfriend to have. Grace couldn't understand it. *"Maybe Mom thinks Damien will tarnish the bond we have since we're so used to being a team of two. Or maybe she really does see Damien as a great guy and just isn't ready for me to grow up and have an actual boyfriend."*

Suddenly an eerie feeling came over Grace, who was still sitting on the park bench watching the parade while Leon and Damien stepped away to converse about school and plans for later that night. As she watched the last line of majorette's dance by she glanced over at Damien and Leon, and she was met with Leon staring and grinning at her. Uncomfortable, she immediately looked down at her phone. Damien was talking to Leon but was also captivated by the final dance of the majorettes and the conclusion of the parade. He didn't even notice his roommate's leer. Grace immediately thought of the counsel from her dad. One of the things he taught her was that if a guy is trying to get a girl that's already taken, he may try to embarrass the current spouse or girlfriend in order to make themselves appear superior or more appealing than them. He told her to always stay away from guys like that because they will do anything-anything- to get what they want.

Leon's reputation was no longer just a reputation, but a living, breathing, creepy fact. *"How could he just disrespect his friend like this?*" Grace thought to herself. Feeling almost violated and not wanting to make any more eye contact with Leon, she decided to text her best friend, Imani while Leon and Damien finished their conversation. Imani and Grace had been best friends since seventh grade. They met during tryouts for the volleyball team at their middle school and have been like sisters ever since. Now seniors in high school, they are very much alike, but also very different. Imani was happy that her best friend finally had a boyfriend. She would often tease Grace that she was going to be an old woman with thirty-five cats, one for each guy that she turned down a date with since they were in middle school. Damien was Grace's first real boyfriend, while Imani had gone through a few, and that is where their differences came into play. Imani could never understand why Grace was so picky, especially since she was crazy beautiful and could have any guy she wanted. Grace didn't want to date casually, she felt it was a waste of time unless it had a strong possibility of leading to marriage. Imani did not agree with Grace's convictions in that area, which caused them to consistently disagree and argue on that topic. Imani felt that Grace was being way too strict, not allowing herself to be a teenager. She thought Grace should live a little and enjoy the cute guys out there. Grace, on the other hand, didn't want to waste time jumping from relationship to relationship just because they had cute faces. She longed for a relationship with someone who wasn't just attractive, but had vision, loved God, valued her, and wanted marriage in the future as well. This was absurd to Imani, but for Grace, it made perfect sense. Grace was told many, many times that she was wise beyond her years. People often told her that she didn't act or think like a seventeen-year-old.

Grace quickly typed out a message to Imani, "hey girl, WYD? I missed you at volleyball practice today, where were you?" Imani's reply came quickly, "Yo!! What's up!? Girl, I had 0 energy, and it kept feeling like I had to throw up. Also, I had this stupid headache; I didn't know what was wrong with me, so I just went home after third period. I was going to text you when I left, but I didn't even want to look at my phone. That's how badly my head was hurting. I'm feeling better now, I may have worked myself too hard at practice yesterday. WYD?" Grace was glad to know her friend was feeling better and started to type a response, "Dag girl, glad you're good now! Well, I'm at the church's parade with Damien, and tell me why his roommate…" Grace's reply is interrupted by the black screen of death.

"Stupid battery!!" Frustrated that her phone died in the middle of her conversation with Imani. Since that was the only thing distracting her from the discomfort she felt around her boyfriend's roommate, she walks over to Damien and Leon. "Hey Damien, sorry to interrupt, but I think I'm ready to go home now. Is it okay if we leave?" She didn't want to cause drama, so she elected to tell Damien about the uncomfortable stares from Leon once they were alone in the car.

"Is it okay if I catch a ride with you too?" Leon asked. Annoyed at the possibility of enduring more strange stares from Leon, Grace tries to quickly give Damien a look to tell him that she was not comfortable with giving Leon a ride, but Damien's face turns very quickly from calm to disturbed.

"Dude, how did you get here? I thought you drove."

Smiling, Leon responded "Nope, I walked. Needed the air, I was visiting my aunt, she lives right down the street. Remember I told you about my uncle that died not too long ago? I try to go over there every now and then to keep her company. I remembered you told me you'd be here tonight, so I decided to slide through and meet your girl I've heard so much about. Plus, my aunt kept trying to feed me these weird concoctions she calls food, so I needed to get out of that house. I just need you to take me back to her house if that's cool with you, it's getting pretty chilly out here."

"Yo, I don't know why you decided to wear shorts in October, this is Maryland dude, the weather changes faster than your girlfriends," joked Damien.

"Aha, you got jokes tonight huh, don't get your feelings hurt in front of your girl."

"Please, you couldn't hurt my feelings if I paid you."

"Dude, with your work-study salary, you couldn't pay me to do anything."

Bursting into laughter, Damien and Leon looked over to see Grace staring back at them in disbelief.

"Are y'all done?" Grace asked with a fake smile, trying not to alert Damien of her true feelings quite yet, but annoyed at the idea of enduring Leon's presence for another minute. She just wanted to get the drive with him over with so she can finally tell Damien about his creepy friend. Picking up on the façade Grace is putting up, Damien tells Leon they can take him back to his aunt's house and they all head toward the car.

As they're walking, Grace sees a familiar face running toward her. As the person gets closer, she realizes it's Leah, one of the majorettes from the parade, and is also one of Grace's students from her youth group at church. Even with volleyball, literary club, golf, and the other extracurricular activities Grace was involved in, she still made time to teach the Young and Free youth group at her church on Sunday evenings. For kids ages ten to thirteen, the group offers safe alternative activities that they can engage in while learning who they are in Christ and who they're called to be. Grace's students love her ability to relate to them, and they definitely look forward to those Sunday evening activities. She encouraged Leah to become a majorette because she recognized the natural gift she had for it.

"Hey Grace, did you see me dance?"

"I sure did, you killed it, Leah! I am so proud of you."

Leah blushed. "Thanks, Grace! Who are those guys?" she asks, referring to Leon and Damien as they get into Damien's car.

"One is my boyfriend, the other is his friend."

"When did you get a boyfriend, and does Ms. Tasha know about this?" Leah jokingly asks.

"Yes, mother, she knows, and don't worry about that, nosy. Anyway, Leah, good job tonight! I have to go, see you on Sunday!"

"Ha-ha, okay Grace, we're keeping secrets now, I see how it is. See you Sunday!" Leah runs back to her family, and as Grace walks to the car, she catches Leon sitting in the back seat, staring at something else. As she follows his creepy stare, she realizes he's not looking at something, but someone, and that someone was Leah. Grace was disturbed all over again. It was one thing to catch him staring at her, but to catch this sophomore in college staring at eleven-year-old Leah ignited a fury within her. What Grace saw was not just a stare, it said to her *I like what*

*I see, and if given the opportunity, I'll act on it.* Leon went from being a flirty, disrespectful roommate to a predator, instantly.

The closer Grace got to the car, the sicker she felt, and the more she wanted to get home and get away from Leon.

As she got into the passenger seat, she hears Leon asking, "Who was that?"

Frustrated and disgusted, Grace responds with a short "A girl from my church." Wanting to change the subject very quickly, Grace asks Damien if he enjoyed the parade.

"You know, I did, it was a lot of fun. Hearing about all of the great things your church has done and seeing all of the talents was pretty sweet. Thanks for inviting me."

"Good, I'm glad you did," Grace responds with a satisfied smile on her face. Determined to maintain her front until Leon is out of the car, Grace asks Leon if he enjoyed himself.

"I sure did, it was pretty interesting, at least what I caught of it."

"Good," Grace responds with a tight smile, glancing back at Leon. During that glance she sees Leon moving from behind Damien's seat to behind her.

"My legs are too long to sit behind Damien, he has me all squashed back here." Feeling oddly uneasy at Leon's excuse for the move, Grace looked over at Damien to see if he is as uncomfortable and bothered as she is, but Damien is suddenly a distant, blurry image.

# Chapter 3

From the echoing whimpers to the scattered chatter, Grace could tell that she was no longer in the passenger seat of Damien's sports car. Disoriented, it felt like that time she had the stomach flu; only this was a million times worse." Her head was spinning; she was nauseous, dizzy, and disoriented. All she could hear was the chatter from what sounded like a lot of girls, but she could also hear faint whimpering or groaning noises, she couldn't tell which. Still coming to, Grace wondered, *Where in the world am I and where the heck is Damien?*

Unable to see clearly, Grace decided to feel her way around to see if she could recognize anything familiar. *Maybe I'm dreaming;* Grace thought to herself. *Why can't I see, and why do I feel so awful? And where is Damien?* As she began to feel around on the hard floor beneath her, she realized her reach was severely limited. Pulling her arms again, she realized she was restricted because there was a chain handcuffed to her wrist. That chain felt like it was attached to some sort of pipe.

*Oh, my God! What?! Did Leon drug me? Have I been kidnapped?!? But why!?* She wondered, panicking, then beginning to cry in that dark, unknown area.

"Hello?" she cried out. "Hello, can somebody help me?"

"Be quiet!" a voice snarls back at her. "You're going to get into trouble, just be quiet. They're gonna hear you!"

Trying to focus her eyes, Grace realizes that the angry voice was coming from what sounded like a young woman just a few feet away. Suddenly, Grace went from fear to utter terror as her mind began to race, and a million thoughts tore through her mind. *What kind of trouble was the other girl referring to, and who were they, anyway? Leon and his friends? How long have I* been here? Why am I here, handcuffed to a pipe? Who would do this to me? Leon? Damien? Or has Damien been kidnapped as well? Maybe he's in another room. Did Leon drug and kidnap both of them? Did he just kidnap me and kill Damien? As Grace's vision became clear, she realized that it was not just her vision that prevented her from seeing her surroundings. The room was nearly pitch black; the only source of light was coming from underneath a door about ten feet away.

Grace felt as though she was in a horror movie. She thought, This cannot be happening to me; this isn't happening to me, right?!" She hoped it was just a nightmare. Maybe I ate something I shouldn't have last night, or maybe I watched a Lifetime movie with my mom before I fell asleep." Yet the more she wondered and considered possibilities in her mind, the more discouraged she became. The last thing she remembered was driving in Damien's car and, they were headed to drop off his creepy friend, Leon. As she replayed the thoughts in her mind, Grace wondered if she'd been lied to, set up, kidnapped, and imprisoned by Damien, even though she had no idea why he would do something like that. All she was certain of was that she was handcuffed to what felt like a pipe connected to the wall next to her, there were other individuals in the room, and at least one girl had already introduced herself by telling her to silence her cries for help. Apparently, this girl was terrified of what "they" would do to them. Still unaware of who "they" were, Grace was definitely not eager to find out. Instead, she thought, Maybe I still have my phone somewhere, I can call my mom, I can call 9–1–1, I can be out of here in no time." Then she remembered. When she got into Damien's car, she put the phone inside her purse, then put the purse on the floor between her feet. She also remembered that it had gone dead while she was texting Imani. She was planning to ask Damien if she could use his car charger. Her mother was a worrier and having a dead cell phone was not acceptable to Tasha. She needed to be able to get in touch with her daughter and Grace needed to be able to reach her as well. Suddenly the small amount of light coming from underneath the door had gotten wider and brighter, and a man and woman stepped into the room. The man was average height, slightly overweight, pretty attractive, with medium brown skin and curly hair. He was dressed in a long white t-shirt and gray jogger pants, with wheat Timberland boots on. He looked like he was in his mid to late forties. He reminded Grace of her eighth-grade science teacher, Mr. Leedy. She'd had a crush on Mr. Leedy, as did several other female students in his class. The woman who walked in was strikingly beautiful, tall with dark brown skin, maybe in her late twenties or early thirties. She looked like a model, but unlike the Mr. Leedy look-a-like, she was dressed up. Even though it's October, she was wearing a pink miniskirt and white halter top, with white pumps to match. *Maybe, she really is a model*, Grace immediately thought to herself, but quickly dismissed it when she glanced around the room. It was no longer dark and, what Grace saw was unbelievable. Several other girls sat on the floor, leaning up against the pipe. She counted six as she glanced around. A couple looked as young as thirteen, at least one appeared exhausted while another one looked heavily medicated. While half were dressed up, the others had on casual wear. Besides the ones who looked medicated, they all had one thing in common: they seemed unbelievably comfortable, but they also looked lost. A couple of them were asleep, making

Grace wonder how long they'd been there for them to be able to fall asleep comfortably. She felt sick to her stomach when she realized that the model was probably not a model at all but was most likely a prostitute. The Mr. Leedy look-a-like was likely her pimp. *No one dresses like this during October in Baltimore, unless you're working.*" Grace thought to herself. She was young, but she was not completely naïve or unaware of the organized crime that went on in her city.

"Alright, listen up girls, Bella here is going to take the newbie and a couple of y'all to the backroom to get cleaned up, and clothes picked out, so we can take some new photographs. Y'all make sure to make her feel welcomed!" The Mr. Leedy look-a-like exclaimed with a grim look on his face. "Grace," he continued, making eerie eye contact with her. "I'm Rolo, and this is my right-hand girl, Bella. She's going to be taking care of you during your stay here at Hotel Rolo, so if you have any questions or concerns, bring it to Bella, and she'll pass it on to me if she deems it necessary. You and you go get freshened up first before we get the newbie in so she can see how it's done. Bella, go pick them out some clothes for photos and for tomorrow morning." Rolo says, pointing to two of the girls. Grace could see what looked like the outline of a handgun tucked away in his pants. Fear began to creep in even further, and she felt even more sick. *Why am I taking pictures? Why does he have a gun? Why does that girl look strung out? Where am I? What time is it? Did my mom report me missing yet? Where in the world are Leon and Damien? Maybe the police are looking for me.*" Grace frantically thought to herself as tears began to roll down her face.

"Make sure you make them look really sexy, I got some eager new clients ready for them," Rolo added. As Bella walked over to un-cuff her, Grace just could not hold it in any longer, she was too afraid and confused to continue to sit there in silence with the questions running through her mind.

"Miss, can you please tell me what is going on and why I'm here?"

"Miss?" Bella sneered back at Grace. "Do I look like a miss, little girl?"

Fully aware that she was in an awful situation, Grace did not want to waste her time trying to defend herself against this lady. She was not one to allow people to speak to her disrespectfully, but she had a feeling her life was possibly on the line and being snappy and defensive was probably not the wisest thing for her to do at the moment. "No, not at all, sorry. I am just trying to figure out what's going on and what I'm doing here," Grace apologized.

Bella rolled her eyes, then turned to relay Grace's message to Rolo in a very condescending tone. "Hey Rolo, this one right here wants to know what's going on."

"Well, I am so glad you asked, pretty lady," Rolo said, making eye contact with Grace, with a devious smile on his face. He then walked toward them. Grace's heart began pounding rapidly and so loudly that she felt as though Bella could hear it. The closer he got to them; the more frightened Grace became. She immediately began to think of ways to defend herself. Her hands were cuffed, so she had limited options. Her feet weren't bound, and his groin was right there for the kicking. She could see that he wasn't that tall, so it'd be little effort getting her feet up there. Then she remembered that she was cuffed to a pipe, and he had what was probably a gun. Even if she kicked him, it would hurt him, but it wouldn't do much to help her since Bella was still mobile. He would eventually get back up, and she would still be cuffed to the pipe, vulnerable to retaliation.

Grace took pride in being the daughter of a soldier. Although she had no interest in pursuing a career in the Armed Forces, she took to heart some valuable lessons her dad taught her, including self-defense techniques. He never wanted his girls to be in a compromising situation and not be able to defend themselves, so Grace and Tasha were both faithful members of a self-defense group that met at their local YMCA called Never Be A Victim. Ernest had organized and taught it before he deployed. She'd hoped never to have to use the techniques, but considering the situation she currently found herself in, they seemed called for.

Rolo had made his way over to Grace and Bella, and Grace found herself overwhelmed by the scent of Rolo's cologne. It smelled as if he had bathed in it, put it on as lotion and deodorant, then brushed his teeth with it. Grace was surprised she couldn't smell it when he was across the room; it was that intense.

"So, you asked what you were doing here, huh? Well, since I don't like to keep my girls in suspense, and in order to perform a job efficiently, you need to know the nature of that job and what the job duties are, right? Well, you see, like I stated earlier, this is Hotel Rolo, all of these beautiful ladies are my guests, and in order to stay here under the Rolo rate, that is for free and unharmed, you just have to make my clients happy."

# Chapter 4

Leon and Damien, also called lover boys, Romeos, or pimps, were the guys no parent wants their daughter to ever run into. To have someone in their daughter's life who appears to be perfect, but turns out to be every bit of scandalous, well that was every mother's fear. Tasha knew how gorgeous Grace was and how much she stood out. Grace was always telling her mom about the men and boys that hit on her.

Damien's exterior was pleasant and admirable, but on the inside, both he and Leon were greedy, apathetic, selfish, broken individuals. One of their schemes was to get young girls to fall in love with Damien then manipulate them. They had Damien swoop into a girl's life, looking like a well-put-together guy from Howard University. It was his roommate who was an awful womanizer. Damien was to react with disgust toward Leon's behavior, which created for the young girl an image of a man who is respectful to young women and is incapable of hurting her in that way. In reality, he is just the same as Leon, disrespectful and hurtful. It is an evil mind game, but one they have successfully used countless times before. That mind game is their segue into getting the girls to begin performing sexual acts for Damien.

Grace, however, was different. Damien saw that she wasn't breaking anytime soon, so they broke protocol instead. They knew she would make them a lot of money, so Rolo didn't want to wait too much longer. Rolo, well, he was in charge, the most dangerous, evil, cold-hearted, and sadistic individual out of the three. He had even gotten some of his family members caught up in his schemes. Damien and Leon thought he was psychotic, but he got the job done, was reliable, and had an important role in helping to maintain their business, so they didn't challenge him.

He was the main reason it was so lucrative, so they stuck with him. He did not care about anyone but himself, coming to realize that in order to survive in the game, he couldn't care about people, and they can't matter. The girls were just a means to his own success, a product. Their lives, feelings, dreams, purity, and value meant absolutely nothing to Rolo.

Fully aware that Grace's mom knew that she had gone out with Damien that night, Leon and Damien had to make sure any suspicion would not be cast on him. They needed to make sure Tasha's mama-bear radar pointed elsewhere. They knew that when someone goes missing, the police and the victim's loved ones like to investigate the last person or people who were in contact with the victim, so they had a plan to deal with that. When they drugged Grace, they took her purse, which had her keys and cell phone inside. Their plan was to sneak into Grace's home. They didn't need to actually break in since they had her keys, but they did need to find a way into the home undetected by Tasha. Once they were inside, they would use the same chloroform that they used on Grace, enough to keep Tasha out of it through the entire night, hopefully. That way, she would not realize that Grace never came home, redirecting the suspicion elsewhere.

When Tasha did wake up in the morning, she'd have a text waiting for her from Grace saying she had gone to grab some groceries for breakfast burritos and would be back shortly. Damien knew that Grace made breakfast burritos almost every weekend for her mom, so he decided to use the weekend ritual to his advantage. He had even been over for Grace's famous burritos a couple of Saturdays. In order to make the fake text appear believable, it needed to be something Grace would actually say and do. Damien knew Tasha wasn't at full mobility, so he thought maybe she would be asleep or relaxing on the couch watching TV.

After taking Grace to Rolo, Leon and Damien drove back toward Grace's house to execute their plan. They parked the car on Henry Court, a few streets away so neighbors or passersby would not notice them. They got out and headed to Grace's home on Lowry Ave, about a one-mile walk.

It was a fairly quiet walk, however for an October night in Baltimore that was pretty normal. Even though it was a Friday night, people celebrating the end of the workweek were inside, whether hanging out with friends somewhere or just at home watching movies. The chilly weather was avoided as much as possible. As they walked, Damien felt an eerie feeling, something he had never experienced before. It was almost debilitating, enough to cause him to stop dead in his tracks.

"Dude, what is wrong with you?" Leon asked, annoyed by Damien's abrupt stop, as he knew they were in a time crunch. They needed to make sure they got to Grace's house before it was too late in the evening, to prevent Tasha from becoming suspicious. If Tasha was still awake and her daughter was too late coming home, she'd get worried and attempt to contact her. They knew that if Tasha was even a little suspicious the night before, it would only grow once Tasha figured out Grace was missing. Although they almost had a foolproof plan, they wanted it to stay foolproof and not take any chances.

"Yo, I feel weird, like extremely weird, like we shouldn't be doing this weird," Damien explained.

Leon's face immediately turned from a concerned demeanor to outright anger. "Dude, are you serious right now, like right now?! You feel like we shouldn't do this?! Yo, what do you mean, we've already done it, now we gotta finish it! Why are you acting brand new like we haven't done this before, did you forget?! This is who we are, this is what we do! Now get yourself together or" Leon paused "just get it together bro, we really don't have time for this!"

Damien knew what that meant. If the others thought that one of the lover boys had gotten soft, fallen in love for real with the girl, or bailed out on their mission, he would be killed, without question. There was no room for someone who decided to grow a conscience. They couldn't afford it, the risk was too great, and that individual would then become a liability to the entire operation. Leon and Damien were really close friends, so Damien thought it would be a lot harder for Leon to do him any harm, but he knew it was not impossible because Leon was not wrapped too tight, and Damien didn't put anything past him. Leon really wanted him to snap out of it so he wouldn't have to take extreme measures against his friend. Damien was pretty sure their friendship wouldn't prevent Leon from doing what he felt he needed to do in order to protect their illegal business.

"You don't feel weird at all, not even a little?" Damien asked Leon, curious to see if he was the only one that suddenly felt strange, and to test Leon to see if he was just playing the tough guy in that moment.

"I feel weird every time we do something like this, but feelings don't make money, so I chalk it up and throw that crap away. You gotta push past that and block it out, or you'll be sitting in a mental institution somewhere, regretting your existence and caught up in feelings. That's also why I take my medicine," Leon added with a smug look on his face as he pulled out a tightly rolled joint. "Been trying to get you to get on board."

"Nah dude, I'm good, you know I don't mess with stuff that alters my mind, I like being in control of my mind and my will," Damien said, earnestly refusing Leon's offer.

"Okay, do what you do, but stop crying and let's go, we are wasting way too much time having pillow talk."

Damien laughed, but that uncomfortable feeling was still present. Ignoring it, he forced himself to just disregard it, and they headed to Tasha's house.

Five minutes into their walk he noticed what appeared to be a homeless family sitting on the corner of Rochester and Linholm holding a sign, panhandling. There was a man and a woman, and judging by their faces, they seemed to be in their early thirties or late twenties. The woman was holding a tiny baby. The sign the man was holding read "Newborn baby, No food, No money, recently evicted family of three, ANYTHING helps." Although it was dark, Damien could see the desperation gleaming from their faces, they didn't have to say a word, Damien felt unusually compelled to lend a hand.

In just a matter of minutes Damien felt like he was falling apart, from the feelings of guilt at the car to the unusual urge to help this homeless family, Damien didn't know what to do or how to handle these thoughts and feelings. He hadn't felt like this in years. He was used to being selfish and emotionless, it's what protected him from caring about the lives he had destroyed. Everything Leon explained to him, Damien already knew. They were the same. Both selfish and loveless, yet for some reason,

Damien was not feeling like Damien that night. When he read that sign, he felt incredibly burdened. He couldn't ignore that family sitting in the cold holding that newborn baby, like he had done plenty of times in the past. This time he felt like a magnet two inches away from the refrigerator. Maybe it was because he was orphaned as a child, but he had bypassed many homeless people in the past. Maybe it was because he already felt uneasy about this plan, or maybe he was using this family as a distraction because he really didn't want to finish the plan. Regardless of the reasoning, he couldn't deny this sudden urge to help this family. Reaching into his pocket, he pulled out a wad of money wrapped in a rubber band. Damien moves toward the family, trying to unravel the wad so that he can give the family the hundred-dollar bill on the outside of the roll. He knew that it would at least give them a two-night stay in a motel, with some fast-food money to spare. It would be a rundown motel, but at least they wouldn't be out in the cold. Realizing that Damien was drifting away from their path toward the family, Leon grabbed him so violently that it caused him to drop the money.

"Dude, are you serious right now!? Were you really about to give those bums some money? What the heck is going on with you tonight? All of this sissy stuff is getting out of hand. First, you're trippin' about finishing our job, now you're about to give some panhandlers some free money? Don't you realize they're running a business bro?!" Leon shouts.

"First of all, you need to calm down before somebody hears you dummy, second of all, I am not one of these females you've tricked, and third of all, my mag is just as full as yours," Damien said, referring to the 9 mm handgun he had tucked away in his pants. Leon was pretty large, he was about 6'3", 220 pounds, yet Damien was not intimidated by Leon's build, even though he was constantly attempting to throw his weight around to bully Damien. Damien was well aware that he'd probably lose in a physical confrontation with Leon, but he didn't care. He always stood his ground because he never wanted to allow anyone, especially Leon, to push him around. He also made sure that he always kept his handgun on him, it wasn't just due to the nature of the business they were in, but if it ever came down to it, he'd pull the trigger before he got into a fight he knew he couldn't win with Leon. The fact still remained, Leon and Damien were good friends, yet Damien perpetually kept his guard up. Leon was a little more passionate, apathetic, and scandalous than Damien was, so he made sure he always kept one eye open.

"Nah, dude, you need to come back to reality, you're being sloppy right now. Think about it! If you walk over there, when it comes out that Grace is missing, don't you think those bums are going to remember two dudes walking late at night close to her house? And if they do a sketch, depending on the recollection of the bums and the sketch artists, they may be able to draw you up real nice and accurate, and guess who's going to recognize it, dummy? Her mother! Her friend Imani! Any of the social media friends, because I'm pretty sure Grace has been posting pictures of both of y'all together. Actually, I know for a fact that she has. You were about to give possible eyewitnesses some money and possibly your fingerprints as well. I know money may have plenty of fingerprints, but you just never know these days! You're just all kinds of soft tonight."

Deep down Damien knew Leon was right, he couldn't risk being seen. He was also puzzled that Leon said he knew for a fact that she'd posted pictures of him on her social media page. How would he know that? But Damien doesn't say anything, he just concedes and continues on their original path, leaving the money on the ground. They continue on to Grace's home and away from the homeless family. Bothered by his disappointment in himself for not giving that family the money, Damien looked back but was surprised to see the man now holding the baby and the woman writing on the sign. Curious to know what the woman was writing, Damien planned to turn back around avoiding Leon's detection. He was not in the mood for another one of Leon's speeches. He planned to look back in a few seconds to see what she had written as he was curious to see why she was changing the sign in the first place. On his second look back, the woman was now holding the sign. With the poor lighting from the streetlight, Damien found himself squinting to read the words. His eyes finally focused and he could make out the words "We're all in need of a little grace, anything helps."

*Grace?* He thought to himself. *This is not happening.* It felt like a blow to his stomach, *out of all the words they could've used, they just had to use that one. It wasn't just the word grace, it was the entire saying. I've seen that somewhere before, but where? And why did she choose to put that up now?* He was feeling creeped out. He thought, *maybe it was supposed to be a way to play on people's emotions, mixing in biblical words with their sad faces, so they feel compelled to give them some money.* He was completely baffled by what just took place, but he decided to continue with the plan, and dismissed it as a mixture of coincidence and a bad day.

# Chapter 5

As they approach the porch armed with ski masks, gloves, and their 9 millimeters, they looked at the windows closest to the ground for any sight into Tasha's home. They needed to make sure she was indeed sleeping, and if not, they needed to find a way in where they would be completely unnoticed. There was absolutely zero room for error, there were many things that could go wrong and ruin their plan. If Tasha found out that she was drugged or realized that someone had broken into her home, or if it looked like Grace hadn't made it home that night, the plan would go up in smoke. So, they needed her to fall asleep like normal, or at least to think she'd fallen asleep on her own. Nothing could look suspicious at all. If she wasn't asleep yet, they preferred to wait for her to fall asleep, or they needed to be extremely quiet, find a way to sneak up behind her then drug her, then place her in her bed as though she had fallen asleep on her own.

This was the part of the plan they weren't really comfortable carrying out, because too much could go wrong if she was awake. Even though Tasha shouldn't remember being drugged, at least that's what they hoped, and that's what Rolo told them. Though a huge part of them didn't fully believe that, it just didn't make sense. They preferred that she fell asleep on her own. They were not amateurs and they knew they had to consider the power of the human mind. What if she realized that she didn't really fall asleep in her bed? What if she has a nightly ritual that she refuses to deviate from, and when she wakes up, she realizes that she hadn't completed it? Their biggest concern, was if the drugs wore off prematurely, and she woke up at 2 am to find Grace was still not there? These questions and possible scenarios were considered going into this plan. There were four windows on the first floor in front of the house, all of which were completely covered and shielded with privacy blinds. Tasha did not play around about the privacy of her home. Who could blame her? A burglary had occurred just a few houses down, so she decided to secure her home. Getting window coverings was the first step, so people could no longer just peer into certain parts of her home. The next step was a home alarm system, with an installation appointment set for the following week. Grace had mentioned the planned installation to Damien, leading him to realize that the job had to be done before the alarm was installed.

As they walked around to the back of the home, they found one window with a slight curtain opening, providing them a small but clear view into the living room area. It looked as though it was mistakenly left open. The house was a ranch style, with all of the bedrooms on the same floor as the living space. The window showed that it was pitch black in the entire home, except for a nightlight in the living room. Damien smirked, *Tasha has another burglar-proof trick to learn, since she's alone, she should have definitely left some lights on to deter any possible crooks.* Crooks like him and Leon. He was kind of disappointed that their plan seemed to be working. The view prevented them from having to play a guessing game, because the lights being off told them that she was indeed asleep or at least getting ready to go to sleep. Both were good scenarios for them, the former being the most convenient. Taking Grace's key out of his pocket, Leon took another step toward the back door. They both took one last look around to make sure they weren't being watched. The coast appeared to be clear, so he slid the key into the keyhole, slowly turning it to the left. Once it was unlocked, Leon quietly turned the knob and opened the door as slowly and as quietly as he possibly could. It was unnerving to both of them. Although they were pretty much career criminals, it was not easy to break into someone's home, because they never knew what was inside waiting for them. This was actually the first time they had broken into a home to drug someone, so they weren't even sure how it was going to play out. As they entered the home, they stepped into the kitchen, closing the door very quietly behind them. They took a moment to look around and to listen for anything that indicated where Tasha was. There was absolute silence, no TV, no shower, no talking, nothing. It was completely silent, a good thing in their eyes. It hopefully meant that Tasha was asleep.

They decided to go check the bedroom area first, Damien knew they were to the left. He had never been in Grace's room, but since he had been over to the house several times over the last couple of months, he knew the layout. All of the bedrooms and hall bathroom were to the left, and to the right of the kitchen were the stairs that led to the basement. The house had three bedrooms: Tasha's, Grace's and an office that was also used as a prayer room. The prayer room was dear to Ernest's heart before he was killed. He wanted to make sure the family had a designated place to go to spend time with God, a place not associated with everything else in the home. Grace had actually mentioned to her mother that they shouldn't have allowed that room to be both office and prayer space, because it wasn't Ernest's vision for that room. They disagreed on it, Tasha argued that with her new position as a graphic designer, she needed a place to work and every other place in the home was too distracting for her. The prayer room was where she found the most peace. Tasha never had to work before; they'd based their way of life around Ernest's salary. She had education in graphic designing, but because they lived within their means and didn't overspend, Tasha just decided to stay home and volunteer with various ministries. She'd donated her graphic designing talents all of the time, for several fundraising events, outreach flyers, and she built websites for businesses, she just loved designing, but never had a career in it. Not working allowed her to use the time to do what she loved, serving people. After Ernest passed away, Tasha needed to bring income into the home, so she accepted a position as a graphic designer at a software company. She absolutely loved it, and she loved that she was able to work remotely. She was so thankful that although she had to work, it was doing something she loved.

As they crept down the hall toward the bedrooms, they could see a light coming from under one of the doors.

"Yo, I hope that's just another night light," Damien whispered to Leon, still feeling uneasy about the plan.

"Right!" agreed Leon. Hoping that the light didn't indicate that Tasha was still awake, they proceeded down the hall. The first room on the left was the bathroom, the next room had the light coming from underneath. As they approached the door, Leon nervously turned the knob, hoping not to startle Tasha and bring attention to her uninvited guests. The turn felt like it took forever. He opened the door just wide enough to peer inside. The bed faced the door, which allowed them to immediately spot Tasha, who was, as they'd hoped, sound asleep in her bed. Finding her already asleep lifted a massive burden off them. Now they were able to carry out their plan smoothly. There was no need for them to put her to sleep, they just needed to keep her asleep in case she decided to get up in the middle of the night looking for Grace. Hoping that the chloroform would do the job and help keep her out of it until morning, they quietly opened the door, and was immediately greeted by the overwhelming scent of lavender. They walked into Tasha's neatly kept bedroom and realized that the light showing under the door was coming from the muted TV. Tasha was snoring lightly, wrapped in her floral comforter, she was laying on her left side facing the door. As they got closer, Damien spotted an essential oil diffuser sitting on her nightstand, which explained the strong scent of lavender. As he took a closer look, the smell wasn't the only thing that captured his attention. On the diffuser was an inscription in beautiful italicized print with the now-familiar saying, "We all need a little grace" and scripture reference Ephesians 2:8. The full verse, *For it is by grace you have been saved, through faith-and this is not from yourselves, it is the gift of God,* was written underneath it. No wonder the words on the sign were so familiar, he had gone with Grace about a month ago to a Christian bookstore downtown to pick out a birthday gift for her mom, the gift was that diffuser.

Damien's heart sank deep into his chest. First, the rather strange sign from the homeless lady, now the exact same saying was right in his face, right there on Tasha's nightstand. And that very uneasy feeling back at the car, that feeling that he should not follow through with this. Damien's mind was racing a million miles per minute, he couldn't understand what these chain of events meant, if they meant anything at all or if he was just being paranoid because they were breaking so many laws. Kidnapping, breaking and entering, human trafficking, sexual exploitation of a minor, child pornography, and the list went on. Maybe fear was driving these events. *Am I so out of it that I'm hallucinating and just imagining all of it? Maybe I didn't see the sign from the homeless lady. Maybe the scripture on the diffuser isn't there. Did I get contact from Leon's joint? Am I high?* Damien had totally forgotten that he was standing over Tasha and time was of the essence. She could wake up at any moment and identify them. If that happened, she'd be a liability and they'd have to get rid of her, something Damien had never done, but Leon on the other hand ...

"Dude!" Leon whispered, angry and impatient. "What are you doing?"

Damien snapped out of his trance, reached into his pocket and pulled out the bottle of chloroform and a rag. Rolo assured them that the chloroform would most definitely help keep her asleep until the morning if she was already asleep when they gave it to her. As he began to soak the rag with the chloroform, Damien's uneasiness returned. Frustrated and angry that this kept happening, he ignored it and gently placed the chloroform-soaked rag to Tasha's nose and mouth for a few seconds. She didn't budge. When he removed the rag, her head fell slightly limp on the pillow.

"Looks like it working, now let's get out of here," Leon anxiously whispered. Damien put the chloroform and rag back into his pocket, and together they left the same way they came in. Quietly. They closed the bedroom door, and they made sure they locked the back door. For Damien, the walk back to the car was long and agonizing. He had never been bombarded with so many thoughts, his conscience never really bothered him before. He actually felt for a long time that he didn't even possess a conscience, he could do as he pleased with innocent girls and feel no remorse, but this time he felt something. It was strange, different, and for some reason, this particular situation was beginning to eat away at a conscience he didn't even know existed, but why? *Why now?* And, was he really hallucinating as he tried to convince himself, did that phrase carry some kind of significance, or was it all just a coincidence? As a man who determined in his heart a long time ago that God, if He existed, really didn't love him, couldn't love him, he quickly dismissed the idea that it was God messing with him that night. From a traumatic childhood to his current chosen lifestyle, he felt God couldn't have anything to do with him, that he was useless and doomed to hell, if there was one. He had long felt that there was absolutely no way that God would want anything to do with him. *I've caused so much havoc, ruined so many lives, betrayed so many girls,* he thought. *Why would God love me or even see me as worthy of being loved?* Because of that mindset, Damien decided that since God wouldn't want anything to do with him, he definitely didn't want anything to do with God.

# Chapter 6

"I am not a prostitute!" Grace yelled at Rolo, tears welling up in her eyes. She already knew that Rolo was running a sex-trafficking operation that he so nonchalantly called Hotel Rolo, but to hear him say it brought immediate fear and disgust. She'd heard stories about local gangs supposedly prostituting girls in the neighborhood and a lot of young girls going missing, she had even gone to an assembly at school that informed the students about the dangers and signs of sex trafficking. Never in a million years did she think she'd be one of them.

"Oh, no, sweetheart, we don't use the p-word here at Hotel Rolo, all of these lovely ladies are my tricks."

*That sounds even more derogatory and degrading than prostitute*, Grace thought, taking a quick look around the room. There were six other girls there. She could see that some of them seemed emotionless, and the rest were visibly under the influence of something. Carefully choosing her next words, Grace decided to ask direct questions, trying not to be too combative. "Why am I here?" Grace asked.

"Well, your boyfriend Damien thought you'd be the perfect addition to our family sweetie, with that pretty little model face and being a virgin and all, you could make us a ridiculous amount of money."

Grace's heart sank. So, Damien and Leon were in on this." One of her worst fears was confirmed. *Not Damien. This is not how my first time was supposed to be. I was supposed to be married and in love, now it's going to be taken from me, for money, from someone I don't even know. How could I have been so stupid and not have seen past Damien's façade? I should have never trusted him, I should have listened to my mother in the beginning instead of trying to convince her that he was a legitimately good guy. I should have known it was too good to be true, right.? But how would I have known that? This is not happening. Not Damien.* Emotionally overwhelmed with the racing thoughts and the realization that she had been kidnapped, to be sold for sex, not just once, but over and over again, and by her "amazing boyfriend" Grace felt sick to her stomach.

"How could you do this to these girls, to me?! I have to throw up," she began gagging, unable to cover her mouth because Bella had not yet un-cuffed her hands.

"Bella, hurry up and get those cuffs off her, then escort her to the bathroom, I don't want throw up all over my floor." Bella reached into her bra, pulled out a tiny key, and kneeled down to unlock the handcuffs.

"Get up and follow me," Bella insisted.

Unable to speak and feeling like everything she'd eaten at the parade was about five seconds away from coming up, Grace got up in a hurry and motioned to Bella that she needed to move quickly, or they wouldn't make it to the bathroom. Rolo moved out of the way so the two could pass.

"And don't think about getting creative," Rolo exclaimed, pointing to the gun shape in his pants.

Unable to focus on anything but the food that was making its way up her throat, Grace ignored Rolo's threat and followed Bella out of the room. As they exited, Grace could see that they were in a house. There were other rooms on the floor she was on, and to the left was a stairwell. She couldn't see everything that was at the bottom of the stairs because the wall blocked her view, but she did notice the front door. They passed two rooms on the right, the very last one was the bathroom. Grace made her way quickly to the toilet and plunged to the floor. As she was throwing up, tears began to flow from her eyes. She hadn't thrown up in years, but the physical pain she was experiencing didn't compare to the emotional and psychological pain she was dealing with. She couldn't believe she was here, she felt like she was having a nightmare and her mom would wake her up any minute, or her alarm would go off. Unfortunately, it wasn't a nightmare, it was really happening.

After Grace finished, she felt even more exhausted. She sat next to the toilet, out of breath and overwhelmed. The boyfriend that she so admired turned out to be a fake who apparently scouted her to be sold for sex. She felt betrayed, angry, heartbroken, afraid, stupid, and vulnerable. As she looked down at her wrists to examine the marks from the handcuffs, she saw the bracelet that her best friend Imani had given her in the summer. She had bought it at a Christian jewelry shop that had just opened downtown, the same shop where Grace got Tasha's diffuser from. Imani knew Grace was a huge jewelry collector, and she really appreciated pieces that had special meaning to them, those that reminded her of God's promises and who she was. She had an entire collection of jewelry, art pieces, and clothing that had some kind of message on them. Imani always joked that she was a walking Bible. This particular bracelet, along with a ring her dad bought for her about five years ago, were two of her favorite pieces. The ring had the scripture Ephesians 2:8, which read *For it is by grace you have been saved, through faith—and this is not from yourselves, it is the gift of God.* He said he gave it to her because it had her name on it, but he also wanted to remind her that her name was meaningful and held a lot of weight, and, because of her name, she was saved. The bracelet from Imani was inscribed with the scripture Romans 8:28 *And we know that all things work together for good to them that love God, to them who are the called according to his purpose.*

Grace was almost immediately encouraged. There was no doubt that she was a Christian, she'd accepted Jesus into her life when she was fourteen, and she sincerely strived every day to be the young woman of God that He called her to be. With the sudden and traumatic death of her dad, Grace found herself questioning her faith, wondering why God would allow that. If it had not been for her mother loving her so much and staying faithful to God throughout that ordeal, Grace would have walked away from Christ with bitterness plaguing her heart. Her mom would constantly recite Romans 8:28, reminding them both that although sometimes unfortunate things happen in our lives, that God allows that to work together for the good. Tasha reminded her that the scripture did not say some things, but *all* things. Through Ernest's death, Grace grew closer to Christ than she had ever been, she was able to tell her story of tragedy and triumph, and she found the courage to share the word and lead others to Christ. She learned that there is something about tragedy that can push you to stop wasting time, stop worrying about other's opinions, and to begin walking in courage. It made her tougher, but for the better. God helped her avoid putting up any walls to protect herself from being hurt, while still trusting Him. That is exactly what she did. In that season, she began to walk in who she was called to be and fell deeply in love with God. Although there were still some healing bumps and friction within the relationship with her mother, she didn't give up, and Tasha didn't allow her to give up. Looking at that bracelet reminded her that she was in that house for a reason, that this situation was beyond her being betrayed. She remembered that *His thoughts are higher, His ways are higher*, which she reminded herself when she couldn't see the bigger picture just yet. She understood that her thoughts are minuscule compared to God's. *Sometimes we only see what we see*, one of Ernest's favorite sayings, also ran through her head. Unfortunately, he would often say it to Grace when she was struggling with faith and trusting God. Too often, she made rash decisions based only on what she could see, her impatience, and her unwillingness to see that God knew best instead of trusting that God had a grand plan and would fulfill that plan within His time. She could beat her fists at God, get angry with Him, walk away from the faith, but she had to withstand that temptation and intentionally trust God in that moment. She made a decision right then and there, next to that funky toilet *I am going to fight. I will not soak in depression. Dad taught me how to fight and taught me how to critically and strategically think. That is exactly what I am going to do, critically and strategically think my way out of this. Mom taught me how to pray and how to allow the Holy Spirit to lead me. I am going to do it all.* She knew that God was going to get the glory in this situation, she just didn't know how, so she began to pray. She had a mission, to get out of there, help get the others out, and to be a light to every single person she came in contact with until she was home.

# Chapter 7

"Alright, little girl, come on. You need to get up," Bella said to Grace.

She looked at Bella, feeling very annoyed that she was so rude to her even though she'd just thrown her entire life up in the toilet, or at least that's how she felt. "Okay, okay. I'm coming." Grace stood up, flushed the toilet, and turned to wash her hands in the sink, which she realized was covered in rust and was obviously not well kept. Wanting to wash her mouth out, but disgusted by all of the rust, she just decided to opt-out. *Maybe Rolo would give me a piece of gum*, Grace jokingly thought to herself. After drying her hands on her pants, since there weren't any paper towels or towels to use, she turned to Bella, who was standing right outside the bathroom, impatiently waiting with a smug look on her face and a hand on one hip. "Okay, I'm done."

"Alright, put your arm out." Grace realized that Bella had taken the cuffs off the pole and had them with her, then the other realization arose, that she was going to be cuffed again. "You're a flight risk sweetie, so we gotta cuff you up." Being a prisoner was one thing, but being chained up made the prison feel that much smaller. It also made her feel like some kind of animal. Armed with her new attitude and outlook on the situation, she just complied, knowing that God had her back. Grace put out one of her wrists and allowed Bella to cuff her. Holding on to the other end of Grace's cuff, they began to walk down the hall and back to the room. About midway down the hall, Grace noticed the downstairs door open and in walked two very familiar faces.

"Leon and Damien" Grace hissed under her breath, rolling her eyes, as anger began to fill her heart. Seeing their faces caused Grace to recall the events that led up to her current situation: all of the lies, the fake persona, convincing Tasha that he was one of the good guys, trusting Damien. All of the time that he spent trying to convince Grace that Leon was no good, that he was a player with this terrible reputation, he was actually in cahoots with him. It was all psychological games, part of the grand plan. *Man, how could I ever trust another guy after this?* She thought to herself, mumbling angrily under her breath. "They are the reason I'm here, no actually, he's the reason I'm here. He is the one I trusted."

"I'm going to need you to stop talking to yourself, little girl," Bella exclaimed loudly to Grace, which caught Leon and Damien's attention. They turned their gaze to the upstairs hallway where Grace was being escorted back to the room. Damien and Grace made eye contact, but this time it was definitely different from the last few weeks. Before today, when she'd look into Damien's eyes, she felt happiness, appreciation, and butterflies; now all she could see was a coward, because in her anger she felt that only a coward would pretend to like a girl just to get them vulnerable enough to be manipulated and sold for sex. But deep down, she knew it was much deeper than that. She knew that everyone has their own deeply rooted issues for carrying out heinous crimes. The crime is just a symptom. Seeing Damien's face brought back all of that anger, regret, and frustration she felt before she began to pray in the bathroom. He knew how important and sacred sex was to her, she'd disclosed that to him. She let him know that she was most definitely waiting for marriage, and that to her, sex was a beautiful gift meant to be shared with the husband that God had for her. She had honestly thought that husband may be Damien, in the future. Realizing that ship had most definitely sailed, she knew the struggle to forgive him may be harder than she'd realized.

"Cowards!" Grace yelled down the stairs to Leon and Damien, with tears of anger in her eyes. Damien immediately put his head down, as if in shame, like he was telling her "I know what I did was wrong, and I am not happy about it." Leon, on the other hand, gave her an eerie smirk very similar to the looks he was giving her at the park.

"Girl, have you lost your mind?! Who told you that you could speak, let alone yell at anyone in this house?!" Bella scolds, yanking Grace into the room, then pushing her to the floor where she had been sitting. "I don't know who you think you are, but you better get it together real quick before it gets ugly." The push caused Grace to hit her arm on the pole that she was handcuffed to. Bella hadn't cuffed her back to the pole yet, and Grace was very tempted to punch Bella right in her face. But she realized Rolo still had a gun and was still in the room looking down at his phone, very unmoved by the fact that his crazy right-hand girl just assaulted her. Even if Grace got past Rolo, she still had to worry about Damien and Leon, who were now downstairs. With Leon's creepiness, she didn't put anything past him, and Damien, she no longer trusted him or even knew who he was, but was he was capable of violence toward her? She didn't know. His response to her calling him a coward showed her that he wasn't comfortable and that something was definitely off, or was it? So many questions arose in her mind. *Was he being manipulated? Is he being forced to recruit girls? Are they blackmailing him? Is he new to this? Or is that still a part of his facade, to get the girls he played to feel sorry for him so he can still look like the innocent one, I mean he did it once already with Leon?*

"You're a little feisty one, huh?" Rolo asks, interrupting Grace's mental investigation into Damien, while looking at her with a very devious smile on his face. "Well, since I broke protocol with you, that's expected. Bella, make sure you cuff her back up, she's got some fight in her. It's unnecessary for right now, but that be a marketable attribute for some of my clients tomorrow. Just have her get fresh in the morning."

As he turned to walk out of the room, Grace fought back all of the words she wanted to spew at Rolo, but she was more confused at what he said about protocol. *Protocol, what protocol? And why in the world did they break it for me?* Although she knew saying anything would probably be a bad idea, she couldn't imagine what Bella, warrior princess, would do to her for yelling at her master or for even questioning him right now. Or what Rolo would do for that matter. So she bit her tongue, yet again. For someone who was used to being outspoken, it was extremely difficult for her not to speak her mind, and not to tell these crazy people off. Bella walked over to her, knelt down, and cuffed her back to the cold pole.

"Vacation is over, sweetie," Bella sarcastically said with a Joker-like smile. Wanting so badly to tell her not to call her sweetie, Grace wisely declined and just gave Bella a fake smile. Bella then stood up and walked out of the room, leaving the door open.

As Grace sat on the floor, she looked around at the other girls. With the light coming from the hallway, she could see around the room a little better. One of the girls was looking back at her with a blank stare, one still looked disoriented, and one of them was asleep. Grace, however, was the only one handcuffed, something she hadn't noticed before. She turned to ask the girl sitting next to her, the one who told her to be quiet earlier, about the handcuffs, only to find her staring. Feeling immediately uncomfortable, Grace asked, "What?"

"I was just wondering what you were thinking, I see you looking around, it's how I was when I first got here."

"Well, I was actually going to ask you why I am the only one handcuffed."

Blank faced, the girl responded, "It's because you're new and probably because they kidnapped you, you're still a flight risk. You haven't been broken-in yet," the girl explained, making air quotes with her hands. "Rolo and the other guys have so much control, the handcuffs aren't needed with the other girls, but with you, they know you're new, and all you're thinking about is getting out of here."

That familiar sickening feeling in her stomach was returning as she listened to the girl. She felt afraid for herself and felt so much empathy for the other girls there. So many thoughts began to flood her mind. *Who knows what these girls have been through, how long they've been there, the trauma they've endured. For what? For some money! To satisfy some perverts hormones?!* Grace thought to herself as she took another glance around the room. The girls were all African American except two of them, who were Hispanic, including the girl she was talking to, who looked to be around the same age as her or maybe a couple of years younger. She was extremely beautiful, with long curly black hair, and she was short and heavy set. She hadn't realized it before, but she looked very familiar as though Grace had seen her before. She had a very inviting face and calm demeanor, a complete reversal from when Grace first got there. Maybe she was so harsh because she was trying to protect herself and the other girls, and Grace was causing too much drama.

"So, what's your name?" Grace asked.

"Bernice," the girl replied. "The girls don't go by their real names in here; they go by whatever name he gives them. They'll try to give you a new one as well."

Assuming she was talking about Rolo, Damien, and Leon, Grace didn't even bother to ask who. "What's the purpose of the name change?" Grace asked curiously.

"Well, for one, it's a way to keep the outside world from knowing who they really are, and two, it's just another tactic to show control. Man, it's all a big mind game with these dudes. They change names, and don't you dare disobey, do something wrong or something they don't like, then it gets real. They threaten you, beat you, torture you, threaten families, deprive you of food and water or a sufficient bed to sleep in. And they enjoy it while making money off the girls. They have no heart, no remorse, no conscience, they're like robots. It amazes me how they can do what they do and not feel anything. Cold-hearted!" Bernice's expression and demeanor went from inviting and calm, to anger, then outright rage.

Not wanting to upset her any further, Grace decided to leave her alone "I'm, sorry if I upset you, I won't ask you any more questions." Feeling such a heavy burden for these girls and realizing that they have probably had a significant amount of psychological trauma, Grace wanted to help them get out of there, and to also get herself out of there, all with God's help. She still was not sure how she was going to make that happen, but she knew God had a plan and when it was time, she'd know exactly what to do.

"It's okay…what's your name?"

"It's Grace."

"It's okay, Grace, it wasn't you. It's this place, this life that's upsetting. Plus, you're a newbie so I don't mind filling you in on the ins and outs, so you aren't completely blindsided like these other girls were. This may be the last day you'll be able to say you were a normal person with a normal life. So, ask away." Bernice assured, flashing a half-smile.

"Okay. Well, I have plenty, so brace yourself." Grace explains with a nervous giggle. "First of all, how old are you and how in the world did you end up here? Did Leon and Damien drug and kidnap you too?"

Bernice laughed, almost hysterically. "Girl, none of the girls in here ended up in this place by being drugged or kidnapped, you're a special case, they must have been really desperate for you. What, are you still a virgin or something?"

Slightly annoyed that Bernice was cracking up at such a personally serious topic, Grace stuttered her response. "Yes, yes, I am. Why, what does that mean to them?"

"Well, to them it means a lot more money. They're able to charge more for virgins because the perverts, well that's what they want, someone no one has had before: a purified beauty. And that my friend is what you are. You also look like some kind of model, are you?"

"No, I'm not. People have mentioned that to me before but I have no desire to be one. It's cool, it's just not my thing." Grace replied.

"Oh, okay. Well, you could possibly make a career out of it, if you ever changed your mind."

Unflattered by Bernice's compliment, Grace forced a smile. For a large portion of Grace's life, she was told that she could be a model because of how beautiful she was. Although she loved the way she looked, she never wanted that to be the only thing people recognized in her, she wanted to make sure people looked past that and saw the real Grace and her love for God, her love for people, her capabilities, her aspirations, her goals, her gifts, not just her beautiful face. So, Bernice's comment just added to the long list of people telling her that she could be a model, or asking is she's ever thought about being one. Grace always responded by assuring others that she didn't want to be a model. None of them, however, ever asked her what she actually wanted to do with her life, so Grace has been on her own journey to prove that she's more than just a beautiful face.

"Well, thanks Bernice, appreciate that, but I actually want to do something involving helping people, not sure exactly what and how that looks just yet."

"Oh, okay, that's cool. Hopefully you can get out of here and be able to pursue that. Don't want you to end up like Bella's crazy brainwashed self, just another one of Rolo's permanent girls. Pretty sure she also had some kind of hopes and aspirations in the beginning. Anyway, back to what I was saying about Leon and Damien. That may be another reason why they decided to snatch you up. A virgin that looks like you, girl, they probably couldn't pass up on that opportunity, too much potential money to be made. And oh yeah, to answer your question about how I ended up here...."

"Wait, hold on, I'm so sorry to cut you off, but can we rewind for a minute?" Overwhelmed with all the information Bernice had spilled out in just a few seconds, Grace interrupted the speed talking. She didn't realize how fast Bernice was talking until she kept going after the Bella remark. "We can't just skate past that whole Bella statement and not address it. What's the deal with Bella? How long has she been here? She used to be trafficked?"

"Oh, my bad. Well according to my *gathered intel,* Bernice explained as she made air quotes. "She's been here since she was like seventeen and she's around twenty-six, twenty-seven now. Yes, she apparently used to be trafficked, and oh yeah, they don't use textbook terminology in here, you'll learn that pretty fast. But, I guess she gained some kind of favor from Rolo, got on his good side, and he ended up promoting her to a higher-ranking position, now she trains the new girls they lure in, or in your case, drag in here," Bernice explained as she continued to form air quotes. "I mentioned she was promoted because now Rolo allows her to at least keep a portion of what she earns, as long as she keeps the girls in line, I guess. How much he allows her to keep is still a mystery."

Feeling overwhelmed and heavy-hearted at the same time, Grace was at a loss for words. Thinking about how long Bella has been here put an immediate dent in her faith and hopes that she'd be out of there anytime soon, but that doubt was soon dismissed when she remembered what her dad used to say to her when she wavered about something she committed to or was trusting God for. He'd first give her this distinct look, a look he seemed to trademark exclusively for that saying. He squeezed his eyes tight, then peered at Grace with this smirk that said *I love you, Grace, but you know you know better.* He always talked to his girls about the importance of faith and how it shouldn't change based on circumstances. "Faith is faith," he'd always say. Those three little words always hit her right in the gut. Her dad really instilled a lot of life's toughest lessons in her while being so loving and contagiously funny. He taught her how to walk in faith in such a faithless world, how to love and trust God even when circumstances didn't have a happy ending. He wasn't aware that he was preparing her for how to deal with his own death.

"People get upset and walk away from God because things don't turn out the way they thought they should or the way they wanted them to," he often said. "But our faith requires us to trust God always, not only when things go according to our plan." Grace was replaying a conversation in her mind that she'd had with her dad about not getting selected to be on the softball team her freshman year of high school. Grace just knew she was going to get to high school breaking records like she did in middle school, but when she found out she didn't make the team, she was devastated. She had this entire high school dream planned out in her head, and softball was a huge part of it. She had a long talk with her dad after that, and that discussion always stuck with her. A couple of months later she began volunteering at a battered women and children's shelter with her mom, and she soon realized that is where God wanted her to be, not softball. If she had made the softball team, she wouldn't have been able to volunteer because the practice for softball was at the exact same time as her volunteer shift at the shelter. Grace had never forgotten that conversation with her dad and that particular situation, because it showed her that God's plan is better, higher, bigger, and perfect, and that sometimes a no is just a yes somewhere else. She was so fulfilled being able to minister to the young kids in that shelter and watching her mom minister to the broken women; it was unlike anything she had ever experienced before. She and her mom volunteered there for two years until God shifted them elsewhere.

"You good over there?" Bernice asked Grace, as she realized she was pretty quiet for a couple minutes.

"Oh yeah, sorry was just processing what you told me and thinking about my dad. Sorry. Finish telling me about your story please."

"Oh okay, you know what, let's save my story for another time, okay?" replied Bernice with a reassuring smile.

"Okay." *Man, she must really believe I am going to be here for a while.* Grace thought to herself. *Lord, please prove her wrong.*

# Chapter 8

"Bro, it's seven a.m., we need to drive over there to send that text ASAP," Leon exclaimed to Damien as he walked into his room without knocking. Not that his sleep was interrupted, because, after last night's series of events, he couldn't sleep. Sleep was actually the last thing on his mind. Damien was sitting at his desk looking out the window, trying to figure everything out. The house that Grace was being held hostage in was rather large and was located in the country, to avoid suspicion since visitors were coming and going regularly. Their closest neighbor was one mile down the road. With six bedrooms upstairs and three on the main floor, Rolo, Leon, and Damien each had a room to themselves. There were four rooms in the basement, and they were utilized for the sole purpose of "business." Bella slept in a room on the second floor with the girls, That particular room was furnished with nothing but four sets of bunk beds.  Leon split his time between the house and his dorm room. Although Damien wasn't an actual student at Howard, Leon was, and that allowed him to recruit, manipulate, and subdue so many young girls. It was the perfect cover. For girls to see him attending a well-respected school like Howard, it was easy to assume he had no ill intentions. The room Grace was being held captive in, which they called the introduction room, is where they put the girls whenever a newbie was brought in, so the new girl can see her housemates, which was all a part of the mind game. It shows the new girls that they aren't alone and it also shows them that their new life is bearable and adaptable since the girls in the room are always the ones who have been there longer. One of the other rooms in the house was the photography and playroom, as Rolo called it. That is where all of the degrading photo taking takes place.

"Yo, first of all, you need to knock before you come in my room, and second of all, you don't need me to drive over there, just take my car and go, her phone is right there on the bed," Damien said. Since the text needed to look like it actually came from Grace's house, they needed to drive over to her house. In case the cops tried to trace where the text came from, they didn't need it bouncing off of cell towers by Hotel Rolo. Not in the mood to argue back and forth with Damien, Leon grabbed the phone from the bed and walked out, leaving the door open.

"Bro!" shouted Damien. "Close my door!!"

Ignoring Damien's request, Leon continued down the hall to the front door. Annoyed and extremely angry at this point, Damien jumped out of his computer chair, raced to the door, then slammed it loudly. He was combatting a rush of thoughts, so many questions, emotions, guilt, and confusion. He had spent most of the night thinking about Grace, the girl, and grace, the word he had seen more often than he wanted to the night before. He didn't understand how his experience with this girl seemed to change the way he thought, the way he saw life, the way he conducted his business, but most importantly, the way he saw himself.

For the last twenty years, Damien had responded to events in his life by running away and drowning his emotions with constant work and avoidance. When Leon introduced him to sex trafficking four years ago, it was another way for him to further ignore his pain, but this time it was directed toward other people. Coercing the girls became easy because he no longer saw worth in people, in life, in anything, because he couldn't see any worth in himself. The life that Damien made up and caused Grace to believe was actually something he only dreamed could be his life. Damien was a foster child and lived in group homes for as long as he could remember. He was an only child who was thrown into the system when he was three years old. His dad murdered his mom in a drunken rage after coming home from a bar, then turned the gun on himself. That was the vivid story told to him by his great aunt Mildred, who came to get him from the homes from time to time. She was the only living sister of his dad's mom. The state wouldn't allow her to have custody of him due to a mental illness she was diagnosed with in her early thirties, so she did what she could to stay in touch and give him a break from those homes whenever she could. She was the only family member who took the time to know him, despite what his dad did to his mom. Instead of taking him in as a victim of his father's actions, his family treated him as though he was a mistake and the direct reason for his dad's awful decision, which was something he never understood. He felt that he was neglected twice, once by his dad and again by his family. When he was fifteen, Aunt Mildred passed away after a long battle with lung cancer. He was broken and felt worthless all over again, confused that he was still in and out of foster and group homes, he just couldn't understand why, for twelve years, no one wanted to adopt him. He was fifteen years old and his best friend and only real family member had just left him all alone in the world. Aunt Mildred had always encouraged him to stay in school and to make sure he got his diploma, so he could get a scholarship to Howard. She told him she always visualized him going there because he was so smart. Because of her vision for him, he decided to make that his dream school. His grades were exceptional, but his motivation was never in the right place. He was smart, but he wasn't driven, Aunt Mildred was his only motivation to excel in life. He wanted to make her happy, so she could say, "You so smart, D."

That is what she would always say when he brought home his work. She wanted him to create his own path, despite his beginning, but when she passed away, he lost the desire to pursue anything. Howard was no longer a goal he desired to achieve, school didn't matter, and graduating was last on his list of things to do in life. His new focus became just surviving. Even though his knowledge and grades exceeded his peers, he decided that he wasn't going to go to school anymore—in his eyes, there was no longer a reason for him to. He no longer had Aunt Mildred in his corner.

Tenth grade is where Damien got a quick taste of the streets, learning how to get by and survive. Because of state laws, his foster parents and group home leaders were required to ensure that the children stayed in school. In order to avoid being constantly preached to, he and a couple of his friends from the group home, Josiah and Tyrell, decided they'd had it with the rules and restrictions. They packed up their belongings one night and ran away in an attempt to make it on their own, free from the constraints that came with group home life. Damien knew they had to make money. In his heart, he wanted to do it legitimately, but as a fifteen-year-old, he knew legitimate work wouldn't come easily, so he'd already determined that he may have to do some things that he wasn't necessarily comfortable with in order to survive. He was prepared. For what? He wasn't sure, but he did know that survival on the streets came at a price. Thankfully, only a few days after leaving the group home, he and his friends found a little under-the-table work at a local barbershop. They didn't make a whole lot of money, about twenty bucks each per week, but for three teenagers living on the street, it was better than nothing at all. The barbershop owner, Mr. Wright, found them one day sleeping at the bus stop in front of his shop.

The entire neighborhood jokingly called him Mufasa, due to his voice, which they described as sounding like James Earl Jones. To add to it, he was a tall, thick-statured man with long, thick loc'd hair, which further sealed the deal. Growing up, Mr. Wright was a foster kid himself and was known for giving out under-the-table work to troubled neighborhood kids when he was able. He didn't just want to give them the opportunity to make money, but he wanted to provide a safe place for them to go in order to ensure they were off the streets and out of harm's way. He knew the dangers that were lurking outside the barbershop doors. He knew there were drug dealers just waiting to recruit them at every corner, or gangs waiting to exploit them for their cause. Mr. Wright only had three rules when he allowed kids to work in his shop. The first was that they were required to attend church with him every Sunday. He would even pick them up from their homes, he just required them to be dressed and ready by the time he got there. Mr. Wright was not only known for his nickname, but also for his faith. People knew him as the Jesus man, and in inner-city Baltimore, that was a rarity. For someone to love Jesus that much, to be that loving, kind, and selfless, and to be that bold and passionate about someone unseen, was not a popular occurrence. So, Mr. Wright stood out in more ways than one. He wanted to make sure he gave hope to the kids in his neighborhood, something he hadn't experienced growing up, until one night when he was seventeen when his foster mother encouraged him one day to attend a youth revival at a neighborhood church. That night, he gave his life to Christ and was never the same. His other two rules were that the kids had to go to school, and once a week they had to do something nice for someone else. He didn't just want them to know how to receive love, he also wanted them to learn how to give it. Mr. Wright understood the power of displaying love and wanted to teach them how to keep the ripple effect going.

Sweeping up hair, taking out the trash, greeting clients, and taking care of any other duties around the barbershop were their daily duties, and for the first month, Mr. Wright even allowed the boys to sleep in a back room in his shop, however, guilt began to set in and he began to feel uncomfortable because he knew they'd ran away from the group home. Damien and his friends were the first kids Mr. Wright helped that were runaways and, after much prayer, Mr. Wright encouraged the boys to return to the group home so he could begin the process of becoming their legal guardian without any issues. They were absolutely thrilled that someone actually wanted to adopt them, they had never thought that would be their story, they thought they would be in the group home until they were eighteen. After four months of home studies and never-ending paperwork, Mr. Wright became Damien, Tyrell, and Josiah's legal guardian. After Elizabeth, Mr. Wright's wife, passed away three years ago from a brain aneurysm, he had lived alone. So, when the boys came to live with him, it was the best thing ever. He and his wife were never able to have children of their own. Elizabeth always wanted to adopt, however, Mr. Wright was never in favor, at least until he met Damien, Josiah, and Tyrell. Something was special about those boys, and he couldn't bear to see them become victims of the streets and hopelessness, because that's what the street life brings. After leaving the group home and moving in with Mr. Wright, Damien had a new outlook on life and school.

Mr. Wright's constant preaching about life and sleeping in the bus stop for those few days made him realize that he didn't want to struggle that hard and that he was making his life way harder than it had to be. He and his friends returned to school, determined to not be high school dropouts, but to finish school, then go to college or enter into the work force after that. Mr. Wright told them that it wasn't the group home's rules they were running from, but it was the fact that the group home reminded them of the abandonment they were experiencing, and they were running away from that. Mr. Wright had very similar rules, they had to go to school, had to be in the house at a certain time, had to do work around the house, and they had to go to church with him every Sunday. Although they went to church, Tyrell was the only one who really enjoyed it. He gave his life to Christ the very first Sunday they went to church with Mr. Wright. Damien and Josiah, on the other hand, were a bit more skeptical and rebellious. They both struggled with the idea of being tied down to a religion. Damien's aunt Mildred opposed organized religions and taught him to just be a good, respectable person. She taught him that heaven and hell were man-made ideologies created out of fear and a desire to give people a sense of comfort prior to death. Before Josiah's mom overdosed, he was taught that Christianity was a bunch of nonsensical tales beaten into the heads of slaves just to keep them in line. Those lessons, plus the violence and abandonment they witnessed in their neighborhoods, made it hard for them to believe a good, gracious God like the one Mr. Wright described was actually real. It was easier for them to just believe in what they could see, such as good people like Mr. Wright. To them, just being a good person was a lot easier and less taxing than being a Christian.

Damien finally had an idea of what it was like to have a dad. Mr. Wright was the best thing that happened to him since Aunt Mildred. Mr. Wright was caring, kind, and patient with him. Even through Damien's constant grumblings about church and Christianity, Mr. Wright was patient with him, but assured him that he needed to make the decision to serve Christ based on truth, and not what was going to make him comfortable. He told him over and over that being a Christian challenged you to be more than just a good person, but to be who God created you to be, and that was more important than trying to be good. Jesus' way is the only good way. Tyrell even tried to talk to him and Josiah about giving their lives to Christ, through countless failed attempts. That difference caused them to drift apart, they were no longer as close as they used to be, and Tyrell was constantly the butt of their jokes. Being adopted by Mr. Wright caused them to see themselves as brothers, so even through their differences, they maintained a love for each other, but could never see eye to eye. Damien and Josiah became closer while Tyrell became heavily involved in church and outreach. His youth group members became his close friends. Tyrell and Damien both excelled in track and field, they were great sprinters, one of the only things that they still had in common. At the end of their sophomore year, they finally decided to put that talent to use and joined the high school track team. By their junior year, they were the fastest members on their track team, earning medals in the one- and two-hundred-meter dashes. In the spring of their junior year, they were preparing for the district track meet, which was being held at their school.

Damien would never forget that day—it was May 9, 2011, a Thursday. Damien and Tyrell decided to just stay at school that day until the events began at 5 pm. They had to be on the field at 3pm, but during sixth period Tyrell realized he'd forgotten his cleats at Mr. Wright's shop. He decided to skip seventh period, his last class of the day and drive over to the shop, about a thirty-minute drive. By this time, all three boys had secured jobs at a local fast food spot, and Tyrell and Damien had even saved enough to buy their first cars. Josiah, though, hadn't been that responsible with his money, and spent most of it on clothes, shoes, and food. Before sixth period ended, Tyrell texted Damien "Aye bro, forgot my cleats at the shop, leaving after sixth period so I can be back by 3." Their coach was pretty strict, and if they were late to the field, he would have them sit the meet out. Tyrell didn't want to risk sitting out a meet as important as districts. Damien responded, "Okay little bro, see you at the field."

That would be the last text Damien would ever send to Tyrell. When Tyrell didn't make it back to the field by three, Damien knew something was wrong. He could feel it. Panic and fear set in, he called his cell phone over and over again. Tyrell loved track and field, and would not miss a meet, especially one as important as districts, plus Tyrell always answered his phone. By 4 pm, Damien was getting ready to get in his car and head over to the shop but was stopped by Josiah running up the bleachers, in tears. The look on his face was something Damien would never forget; it was forever engraved in his mind. Damien already knew what it was. Tyrell was gone. He wasn't expecting the other part of Josiah's story. Mr. Wright was also gone. Apparently, while Tyrell was in the shop picking up his shoes, Mr. Wright was also there cleaning up the back rooms. On Thursdays, the shop closed at noon and reopened Friday morning at 10, so Mr. Wright usually went golfing with his friends from the Men of Fire, his men's fellowship group from church. A few of the members had the flu, so they decided to link back up the following Thursday.

Mr. Wright decided to take that time to clean out the back rooms, because he planned to expand the shop space in order to service more clients. Everyone knew the shop closed early on Thursdays, and Mr. Wright was worried about break-ins by the homeless or drug addicts. He planned to get a sophisticated alarm system but kept putting it off. He would often talk about how high tech it was going to be. No one was sure what happened, but the belief was that Tyrell was killed when he walked in while a suspected drug addict was looking for cash around the shop. At that point, Mr. Wright was probably already gone. When the police arrived, Mr. Wright and Tyrell were both found in the backroom and the barbershop was completely ransacked.

From that day forward, Damien was never the same. Something in him broke. He lost touch with reality, with people. He no longer cared. It hurt more than losing Aunt Mildred, more than not being adopted all those years. He could not understand why the two people in his life who had the biggest hearts, and who fully believed in this Jesus, could be taken from him like that. That day, the foundation was laid for Damien, the sex trafficker. He never returned to school, he abandoned his life, track and field, and Josiah. A few months later, he met Leon.

# Chapter 9

It was now 9:00 a.m., two hours since Leon left to text Grace's mom. He hadn't returned yet, and Damien was wondering what was taking him so long to complete such a simple task. As he was pulling out his phone to call him, he heard some commotion upstairs. He put his phone in his pocket and opened the door to see what was going on. As he looked up to the upstairs hallway, he found Bella escorting Grace to the playroom. She was wearing light blue jean shorts that left nothing to the imagination and a red halter top. Damien was used to seeing the girls dressed like this, and it never bothered him if they were uncomfortable in those skimpy outfits. But this time, seeing the shamed, petrified look on Grace's face made him feel an inch tall. He knew she didn't wear revealing clothing because she didn't like the attention that came with it. Now he was the reason she was being forced to abandon what she stood for. Most of the girls Damien manipulated in the past were or had been sexually active prior to them meeting him. Some had a code of ethics they stuck to until they met Damien, and he defiled their innocence. Most of them also had a history of sexual abuse and trauma. That made it easier for Damien to coerce them because he was able to prey on their trauma.

Seeing Grace made Damien feel sick to his stomach. He knew that once her photos were uploaded, her life would be forever changed. Their current and potential clients on the dark web were always looking for pretty, young virgins, and once her photos were uploaded online, it was just a matter of hours, possibly minutes, before Grace would have her first paying client. Unable to bear the sight of Grace in that outfit and the thoughts of what was soon to unfold, Damien walked back into his room. Pacing back and forth, anxiety and regret overwhelmed him. He hadn't felt anything this strongly since Aunt Mildred, Mr. Wright, and Tyrell died. It was like Grace turned on something back on in him, something that had been shut off for years. He paced back and forth, wondering what was going on with him and why Leon hadn't returned. Then he remembered that he needed to call him to see why he was taking so long to come back.

He knew that something was off with Leon, and that he could not be trusted. Although they were good friends, Damien was still on guard with him. Hoping that Leon hadn't deviated from the plan and done something to Tasha, Damien called Leon. It rang once then was cut short, sending him straight to Leon's arrogant voicemail message.

"You reached Leon, I'll return your call at my earliest convenience. Nah, I probably won't." He tried several times, always getting the same response. Damien was sure that Leon was capable of killing someone, and it was possible that he had done it in the past.

As crooked and messed up as Damien was, he was just never comfortable with taking someone's life. Leon, on the other hand, had a few more screws loose, and a lot less conscience than Damien. Damien decided to text him "Bro, where are you? Hit me up, ASAP." It was Saturday, a high-traffic day for Hotel Rolo. Saturdays brought in around one hundred clients, about sixteen clients per girl. That was business as usual, but today Damien was not his usual self. He stayed in his room, trying to avoid the possibility of seeing Grace again. He actually did not want to see anyone. He tried to sleep to get away from the thoughts going through his head, but he couldn't. He felt insane. It was now 11 a.m., and he still hadn't heard from Leon. He couldn't take it anymore, the suspense was eating away at him. He decided to drive over to Grace's house to make sure Leon hadn't done anything to Tasha. He already knew what he'd say to her, that he hadn't seen or heard from Grace since last night. Damien grabbed his coat and headed to the front door, then remembered he'd let Leon take his car. Frustrated, but too eager to check out his suspicions, he called for an Uber and within fifteen minutes was on his way to Grace's house, thirty minutes east.

While Grace was grateful that Bella and Rolo hadn't made her pose nude, she still felt disgust, shame, and violated to the $2^{nd}$ degree due to the ridiculous clothing she had to wear and the explicit photos she had been forced to pose for. The poses Bella instructed her to do while Rolo took the pictures were tasteless, demeaning, and degrading to say the least. She felt so angry and defiled. There was a reason she didn't dress that way, and now, she'd been forced to. Back in the introduction room, handcuffed to the pipe, and still wearing those revealing clothes, Grace was exhausted. She hadn't slept at all since she was handcuffed all night, and she had spent the majority of that time talking to Bernice, getting to know her, and getting schooled on the life of sex slavery. They also had several conversations about God, Grace had never heard anyone talk about God the way Bernice did. She couldn't stop listening to her speak.

Grace began sobbing. Now, she was in there alone. The other girls were in the basement getting ready for their Saturday clients. Fear set in as she recalled the conversation she and Bernice had the night before about Grace being a virgin and how she was apparently a big hit for them. Bernice told her that Saturday was their busiest day of the week, and the moment Rolo put her pictures online she was going to get her first client.

Unless Rolo already had a buyer in his back pocket, which was a possibility considering what her virginity and looks were worth to them. Bernice told her that they were going to go with whoever was paying the most. Online, the girls would usually sell within minutes to several buyers, so that could prove to be the more lucrative route. Grace began going over the layout of the house in her mind, at least what she was able to capture during her trip from the introduction room to the bathroom and the playroom. She was strategizing several ways she could somehow escape. *Maybe I could find something to make a shank out of, or maybe I could get close enough to Rolo to grab his gun, or maybe I can jump out one of the windows.* The more she thought of ways to escape, the more they began to sound like suicide. She couldn't think of anything lying around the house that could be fashioned into a shank, and getting Rolo's gun may be possible, but he wasn't small, so it would not be an easy task. If she failed, it would result in retaliation. All the windows that she'd seen were covered by bars. It was truly a real live prison and slave camp. According to Bernice, the girls are allowed outside, but only once they've made a certain amount of money for the day, and they were restricted to the fenced in back yard. By that point, they no longer require supervision because the girls are so psychologically damaged, they think Rolo and the other guys are doing them a favor. Bernice told her that was how they kept most of the girls there without physical restraints, the trauma bond. Bernice told Grace all about the trauma bond last night. The girls viewed Rolo, Damien, and Leon as their protectors, and they believed they actually loved them. Most of the girls endured a life of abuse, neglect, abandonment, and lack of love. After the girls are finished with their clients for the day, Rolo and the guys always made sure to give them hugs or some sort of affirming affection while telling them how loved and appreciated they are.

They also buy their favorite desserts on the weekends, contingent upon them doing what the guys called a good job all week. Since the girls had never been applauded for doing good, never been told they were loved or appreciated, despite being raped every day, they thought that being awarded with their favorite things and receiving affection, showed them that they were loved and appreciated, and seeing that it made the guys happy was something to be glad about. At home or in their foster homes, abuse was never followed up with affection, just more abuse. Now that abuse was followed with affirmation and false love, the girls think they are being loved and cared for. Rolo, Leo, and Damien used the girls' trauma to their advantage, even talking to the girls about their past trauma as though they genuinely cared for them.

From the outside, it can be hard to understand how anyone could mistake this for real love, but it happens, and this house was just a small piece of this worldwide plague. As Grace listened to Bernice explain that to her, she was both floored, heartbroken, and compounded with emotions of grief and anger. She also felt a hint of guilt, because she'd experienced so much love in her family, and those girls hadn't. It reminded her just how hurt so many people were, and right in her own backyard. It reminded her of her duty to love everyone, to show the love of Christ, and to witness to those who were lost. It reminded her that there are many broken people. It reminded her of the need for God's truth. It reminded her of the darkness and coldness that consumed many people's hearts. Grace asked Bernice why she'd heard crying when she first arrived if the girls were so comfortable there.

"Oh, she was high on marijuana, and when she's high, she cries," Bernice explained. Grace thought it was weird, but she knew enough about drugs to know that everyone responded differently while under the influence. Bernice explained to her that the girls were usually high, it helped them to numb the pain of servicing the clients on a daily basis.

Grace and Bernice talked about everything the night before, from faith to jewelry, to the other girls in the house. They had even prayed together at Grace's request. After they prayed, Bernice said something to Grace that she would never forget. It was simple, but it seemed very powerful. "You're not just meant to be a light of Maryland, you are the light of the world." Grace didn't understand the inspiration behind the reference, but for some reason, it felt like spiritual whiplash. Bernice didn't do much talking about herself. Grace just knew that her name was Bernice and she seemed to love God. She was also quite intelligent. She didn't seem too thrilled to talk about herself, and Grace just couldn't get a read on her. She dismissed it, and didn't want to push her to talk about something that was most likely traumatic for her. Bernice did fill her in on the others, which Grace thought was sort of odd, that she was so comfortable telling her about everyone else, but not herself. Grace didn't get a chance to talk to any of the other girls that night, they fell asleep while she and Bernice talked. Bernice gave her the backstories on all five of them: Malia was the other Hispanic girl, and she was only twelve years old. Latrice and Brittany were seventeen, the same age as Grace. Tamara was fourteen, and Unique was also twelve. She was the one who had been crying the night before.

When Grace learned their ages, she couldn't believe it. She knew they looked young, but hearing it actually confirmed was sickening. Tamara, Unique and Malia were all from foster homes, apparently, Leon had been their pretend boyfriend. Leon usually scouted the younger girls, while Damien was better at manipulating the older ones, plus he felt scouting younger girls was sick, but he wouldn't dare express those concerns, so he just kept his mouth closed. Latrice and Brittany were both from abused, drug-stricken families. Damien was their Romeo or loverboy. Grace just could not believe that people like Leon, Damien, and Rolo actually existed, in her own life, her neighborhood, and the community that she loved so much. But they did exist, and sex traffickers really existed everywhere. It was no longer just information being presented at school; this was really happening to her. As Grace sat in the room alone, thinking that this may be her last day as a virgin, she started to cry again. *How can I get out of this situation? It seems impossible*, she thought. Her crying turned to weeping and she began to pray. "Jesus, I need you so badly right now, I can't believe this is happening to me, I shouldn't be here, none of these girls should be here. But, I know you are El Roi, the God who sees me. You are here, You have a plan, with You nothing is impossible! Please Lord, don't let these evil things happen to me, send your angels to camp around me, and help me get out of this place today. Fill this place with your presence, convict those responsible for this evil, and please deliver us all, thank you, God, in Jesus's mighty name, Amen!"

Damien had the Uber driver drop him off at a barbershop a few streets away from Grace's house. If anything went down, he didn't want to give the Uber driver the opportunity to link him from Hotel Rolo to Grace's house, so he tried to cover his tracks as much as possible. As he was getting out of the car, the storefront barbershop captivated him. It was reminiscent of Mr. Wright's shop, with the same cultural appeal. The afro, comb, and razor silhouettes decorating the clean, large glass windows prompted flashbacks to the time he spent at the shop with Mr. Wright and his brothers. He actually wasn't too far away from where that shop used to be, it was just five blocks away.

After Mr. Wright's murder, however, the shop was seized by the city then sold. It soon became a restaurant. The beloved neighborhood corner barbershop was no longer Wright Cutz, but Henry's Shrimp Boat. The neighborhood took a hit when Mr. Wright was killed. The youth that he inspired and took time with no longer had a place of refuge. And because Mr. Wright didn't allow drug dealers to sell in front of his store, while he was alive that corner had been drug-free. That wasn't the case anymore. Wright Cutz was definitely missed.

Damien stood in front of the barbershop for a few minutes, thinking about how amazing and selfless a person Mr. Wright was, and how he would be so disappointed in Damien's life's choices if he were still alive. The last couple of days had been extremely draining for Damien. He had a very lucrative business, but he couldn't figure out why nothing made sense anymore. When he saw Grace in those clothes earlier, he felt he'd made a huge mistake. He couldn't even comfortably lust after her. A part of him felt as though he was actually ruining her life. But he couldn't understand what was actually bothering him. They had taken the other girls from a horrible, loveless life, so in Damien's mind, he believed they were doing the girls some kind of favor by seducing and manipulating them, then forcing them to have sex with clients every night and not allowing them to keep any of the money earned from it. *At least we give them some sense of self-worth and a stable place to stay, right? At least Bella takes the girls to the hospital when they get STDs.* Not only were the girls deceived, but Damien was as well. Rolo didn't care about the health of those girls, he just didn't want his "products" spreading diseases, because that could interfere with his money. He'd tricked himself into believing they may have actually been doing the girls some kind of favor, at least they weren't as harsh to the girls as competing traffickers in the area. At least, that's the excuse he'd clung to, a defense mechanism put in place to block out all the evil he had caused and been responsible for. Maybe that was his excuse.

Those guilty feelings didn't just start that morning, they started the moment he met Grace, three months ago in July, at a backpack giveaway for a local group home. Grace's church sponsored it. Damien signed up to be a volunteer. However, he wasn't there to be a good Samaritan; he was there scouting girls from the group home. Because of their brokenness and neglect, they were the vulnerable targets, but when he saw Grace, he decided to go talk to her. Her beauty was captivating, but it was something else that drew him to her. Maybe it was because she was a church girl, and he thought that would be a fun challenge. A new accomplishment, being able to break and traffic a church girl. Or maybe it was because she didn't seem to be craving attention or the fact that she didn't even notice he was there volunteering until he approached her. Damien was used to girls noticing him, he was very attractive to most. The attention was not something he'd ever had to work hard for. Grace not acknowledging his presence sparked a challenge. He was going to get her to notice him. Before approaching her, he snuck a cell phone photo of her and sent it to Leon. "Bro, check her out," the text read. He then walked over to her booth, which was loaded with informational pamphlets about identity and value. There were also goodie bags for the smaller children in the group home.

"Hey, beautiful," were Damien's first words to Grace.

"What's up?" she responded with a forced smile, unimpressed with his cheesy compliment.

"So, you go to this church, the one that's sponsoring this?"

"Yes sir, why? Thinking about joining?" Grace asked with a curious, yet polite, demeanor.

"Sir? Yo, I look like a grandpa or something? And, actually I am. I'm in search of a new church because I'm not really feeling the new pastor at my current one." Damien was impressed with how quickly he thought of that lie., mentally patting himself on the back when he realized he had the attention of this beautiful girl. They talked for the rest of the outreach, about life, God, church, goals, school, and money. He had caught Grace's attention, something no guy had been able to really do before. Apparently she'd caught his as well, because he'd forgotten that he was there solely to find a girl from the group home. It completely escaped his mind. At the end of the night, he realized he had unread text messages from both Rolo and Leon.

After opening the first one, he remembered that'd he'd sent Grace's photo to Leon.

"Shoot!" he exclaimed. The first one was from Leon, and it simply read "$$$$$$$$$$." The next one was from Rolo, "Bro, just got that photo from Leon, make that happen ASAP." He knew exactly what that meant. He had sent Grace's photo to them, and now they expected him to scout her. Sending photos of potential girls was a common practice for Leon and Damien. Prior to sending that photo, he would never have thought Grace would be the reason he would regret it. Damien felt uneasy, something was different. From that day on, he regretted even meeting her. More importantly, he regretted sending that photo, but he couldn't seem to leave her alone. After a month of getting to know each other, they began dating. However, that didn't change Rolo and Leon's plan of getting her on their list. Once he sent that photo, Grace was on their radar, and he couldn't undo it. They weren't allowed to have legitimate girlfriends or be attached to any female in that way. Girlfriends were only a part of the scheme, to trick the girls into thinking Damien or Leon actually cared about them. It was forbidden because it showed vulnerability, weakness, and lack of focus. The moment they began to get attached to someone, it would change their entire perspective, and they wouldn't want to scout anymore. They would grow a conscience, and begin to see girls differently—the way they were supposed to—with love, honor, and respect. Being cold-hearted and loveless was the way they maintained their business. No obligations, no commitments.

Damien and Leon liked to pretend they had equal control with Rolo, but they all knew that wasn't the case. Rolo ran the show, and if Rolo told him to make it happen, then he was going to do what he was told. Damien also didn't like the fact that he was beginning to feel what he perceived to be actual feelings for Grace, along with an abhorrence for his line of work.

Ignoring the change attempting to occur in his heart, Damien decided that Grace couldn't be the exception, and he would proceed with business as usual. He was going to do what he always did with his pretend girlfriends, and for the past two months, he tried. Grace didn't budge. He was amazed that she wouldn't even kiss him. She decided to wait until marriage, not only to have sex but for her first kiss as well. He couldn't penetrate her philosophies, as he called them. He knew once he had her mind, her body would be soon to follow. However, her faith caused her to have this unbelievable foundation that Damien could not crack. She knew who she was. She knew who God created her to be. He reluctantly developed the plan to take her unwillingly once he realized his usual methods wasn't working. Kidnapping was something they hadn't done before, but Damien was determined, and Leon and Rolo both agreed with his plan.

During Damien's ten-minute walk to Grace and Tasha's home, he rehearsed what he would say to Tasha and how he was going to handle her emotions, because by this time she was probably awake, frantically wondering why Grace hadn't returned from the grocery store yet and why she wasn't answering her phone. That is if Leon hadn't done anything stupid.

Leon was supposed to send the text between seven and eight a.m., and it was now noon. Damien really had to put his acting skills to use. He planned to tell Tasha that he hadn't heard from Grace that morning and that he came over to return the wallet that she'd dropped in his car. If Tasha asked him where his car was, he'd say that his roommate was using it, but what if she asked why he wasn't dropped off in front of the house? *What would he say?*

This possibility stumped Damien, and he needed to think quickly because he was almost at Tasha's house. *Shoot, shoot. What should I say, what should I say?* he frantically pondered to himself. *Oh, I got it, I can just tell her that I caught the city bus, the bus stop is right around the corner.* Relieved that he had dodged that bullet, he was now at Tasha's house. Damien was nervous. He was nervous because he was hoping Leon didn't deviate from the plan and hurt Tasha, and nervous that he was about to face the mother of the girl he'd kidnapped. He couldn't believe what he was about to do. Deceit was a normal part of his life, but this time it was slowly eating away at him. He suppressed the nerves and shame over and over, but now he felt as though he was going to explode.

Damien walked up the four steps and reached to push the doorbell, but before he managed to ring it, the front door swung open, and there was Tasha with a frightened and relieved look on her face. He was glad to see her alive, but dreaded what was coming next.

"Damien! I was just thinking about you, please tell me you've heard from Grace?!" Tasha was frightened. It was apparent she was going crazy wondering where Grace was, and relieved because Damien had just showed up.

"No, ma'am. Unfortunately, I haven't. That's why I came over because I've been trying to reach her since about nine this morning. I wanted to bring her wallet that she dropped in my car last night. She hasn't been responding, and I wanted to make sure she had her wallet. When is the last time you saw her?"

"Well, she sent a text at like seven-thirty this morning saying she was going to get some stuff for burritos. I woke up around eight-thirty and saw the text. Then around nine, I started to get worried, because you know the grocery store ain't far at all. It's right up the street in that plaza. So, I tried to call her to see what was taking so long, and it went straight to voicemail. I tried several times after that, to no avail, so I called up to the store. I asked them to look around for her. They told me they searched all over, and she wasn't there. So then I knew something was wrong, I could feel it. I even asked the cashiers if they'd seen her, and none of them had." Tasha began to cry. "So, now I am wondering if she even made it to the store. Then I wanted to call you, but of course, I don't have your number, so that was a dead end. That's why I was so happy you showed up."

Damien's tough-guy facade was being crushed by the second, with every word Tasha spoke, and every tear he saw fall from her eyes.

*What have I done?* Damien asked himself. Out of all of the girls he'd manipulated and schemed, he never had to deal with a distraught, concerned loved one. The others had been abandoned, so many people had rejected and abused them. "Oh man, Ms. Tasha, please tell me what I need to do to help find her. Do we need to print up flyers, call the police, please tell me?" That was Damien's attempt to appear distraught. Actually, he was genuinely distraught, but not because his girlfriend was potentially missing. He was distraught because his girlfriend *was* missing, and it was all his fault.

"I called the police already, they left right before you got here. They told me I need to wait forty-eight hours before I file a missing person's report, but they will be actively looking for her and doing what they can. Which is completely ridiculous!! Do you know how long forty-eight hours is? In forty-eight hours, she could be in another country!" Tasha exclaimed, tears still falling from her eyes. Damien felt Tasha's pain. He was the reason for it. "While you're here, can you give me your number so I'll have it saved in my phone?"

"Yes, of course," Damien replied. Tasha walked over to the kitchen counter. "Did Grace mention anything about any other plans she had for today?" she asked.

"No, she didn't mention anything to me. Are you ready for the number?" Damien asked Tasha while quickly dismissing her question.

"Thanks. I'm calling you, so you will have mine as well."

"Okay, it's ringing," Damien told Tasha as he silenced his phone. After Tasha hung up, he saw two unread text messages, one from Leon and the other from Rolo. He quickly opened the first one, and what he read almost made his heart drop to his feet. Rolo's message read, "Yo, got some high paying clients lined up for ya girl this evening. $$$$$$$$" The next one was from Leon, in response to the many texts Damien had sent him earlier. "Phone was dead."

Something in Damien snapped. Overwhelmed with anxiety, Damien ordered an Uber to take him back to the house. He no longer cared about covering his tracks, he needed to get to Grace. From day one, he knew she was different, he knew she would challenge him to look at himself differently. She didn't even know that, because everything she knew about him was all lies, all a façade of a well put together man. "Wait, how was she going to pay for groceries if she didn't have her wallet?" Tasha asks with a baffled and suspicious look on her face, interrupting Damien's mental guilt.

*Man, I didn't think of that, how could I be reckless like that, I thought I thought of everything. Shoot!* Damien thought as he opened his mouth to respond. "Hmm, that is weird. And she always has that wallet with her, I've honestly never seen her without it, even if she didn't have a purse, she still had that wallet," he said. That wallet was like a second cell phone, she never went anywhere without it. She bought it last year at a garage sale because she loved it so much. It was her favorite color, royal blue and had a weird-looking cat embroidered on it. She had a knack for odd things.

"Something isn't right Damien; something is just not right! This morning, I woke up with the worst headache. I haven't had a headache that intense in a very long time. It felt like one of those drunk college days, hungover-type headaches, from my before Jesus days. Now, my daughter is missing!" Tasha exclaimed as she began to cry again.

"Ms. Tasha," Damien walked over to console her, but she interrupted him.

"Can you pray with me, I just need to pray."

Reluctantly, Damien responds. "Yes, of course." He knows his Uber will be there any minute, and he has to find a way to get out of there, so as to not cause suspicion. They grab hands, Tasha clenching Damien's hands so tightly, he begins to lose feeling in them. But he can feel her anguish, every ounce of it. He could literally feel her pain, her turmoil.

"Jesus, please, I need you, we need you! Please send my daughter home, please protect her wherever she is, and please let no harm come to her. Send your angel to camp around my baby, comfort her, keep her safe, please help her to remember that she is loved and not forgotten, and if anyone is responsible for this I pray that you convict them, cleanse their hearts, and deal with them accordingly. You are perfect, your ways are perfect, thank you for what You're going to do, in Jesus name, amen!"

"Amen," Damien agreed. Feeling like he was going straight to hell after that prayer, he wanted to run out of that house without any explanation to where he was going. "Ms. Tasha, I am going to head over to my dorm, get my car back from my roommate and head back over so we can look for Grace. I will make sure I keep my phone turned up so I can hear it if you or Grace calls. I really hope she's okay, I don't know what I'd do if something were to happen to her."

That last sentence was possibly the only thing he said that was true. He was heading over to Hotel Rolo because he didn't know what he'd do if something were to actually happen to Grace.

"Okay, but do you have to go right now? I mean, we could both take my car and we can scavenge the neighborhood together. Or, I could take you to get your car?" Tasha asked.

"Hmm, I think it would be more beneficial if we spilt up, that way we can cover more ground, and my ride is already on the way." Tasha didn't respond. Damien stared intently at her, waiting to see if she was buying his excuse.

"Okay, that makes sense Damien. Looks like it's a car outside, is that your ride?"

Relieved that second of deadly silence was over and that she had bought his excuse, he headed to the front door. "Yes, that's me. I will be back soon, stay encouraged, and keep praying,

Ms. Tasha," Damien urged, as he headed out the front door, and got in the car. He knew the lingo, but couldn't seem to believe it for himself. Clueless what the possible fallout following his unknown plan would look like, there was one thing he was sure of, and that was that he had to save Grace.

# Chapter 10

"I'm still trying to figure out what I'm going to call you. You remind me of a Tanya or a Keisha. You know, I haven't even uploaded your photo yet, and you already got clients lined up for this evening. I guess Leon already had some in his pocket," Rolo said to Grace as he walked into the room with a tray. It held a sub sandwich, a bag of potato chips, and a water bottle. It appeared to be from Subway. Grace loved Subway, but in that moment, food was the last thing on her mind, especially food from the enemy. She didn't know what was in that food. They could drug her, make her more suggestive to their plans for later that day. She was still tied to a pole in very revealing clothing, waiting for her virginity to be snatched away, then to be passed from client to client. They would be able to do whatever they wanted to do to her, by paying money that she would never see. She was sleep-deprived and her eyes were swollen from constant crying, her wrist was sore and bruised from the handcuffs, and her heart felt completely broken.

*I'm so angry*, she thought. *I have to escape. I can't fail! Why hasn't anyone come to rescue me yet? How could I let a man like Damien into my life? I thought I could actually love him! I thought I might marry him! Why did I even talk to him that day at the outreach? I wish my dad was here! I need him! How could he leave me and mom? I know he would have found me by now if he was still here!! And there's the door again. Those animals just keep coming!*

She'd heard the front door open and close several times over the last few hours and expected it was the rush of clients Bernice told her about the night before. Every time she heard the door close, every footstep made her feel sick to her stomach. Not only was she disgusted with Rolo, Damien, and Leon, but the clients as well. *What kind of people would pay to have sex with these young girls over and over!? Do they not care about their well-being, their families, their mental health. Sex trafficking wouldn't even exist if there weren't clients willing to pay for it.* Then she realized something. *The demand was great because the sin behind it was great. Lust!* She thought about the girls. She saw past their façades and saw brokenness. She could tell they were hurting. To have to be high just to get through the day was heartbreaking. They weren't comfortable as she had originally thought, they weren't accepting, they were surviving. Surviving their current situation is what they were doing, and the drugs prevented them from having to deal with the mental turmoil that came with that life.

Grace had spent the morning battling between waiting for God and doubting God, wondering if she had done something wrong. Wondering if she had ever ignored a sex-trafficking victim and was now reaping the consequences from that. She remembered her dad's words, *faith is faith*, and that kept bringing her back to ground level, trusting God. She felt disoriented, nauseated, and weak. She said nothing in response to Rolo's comments, just watched him with fury in her eyes as he got closer to her with the food tray. Thinking of ways she could use this situation to escape, she quickly dismissed them all, as they all resulted in her possibly getting beaten, killed or both. Rolo placed the food tray on the floor right next to her and she could smell the cologne he had showered in the night before. This time, it didn't smell as strong, and it smelled as though it was mixed with body odor and sweat, as if he hadn't showered at all. Twisting her face in disgust due to the smell, Grace turned her attention to Rolo's clothing, and she realized he was wearing the exact same clothes as the night before. That would explain the smell. He went to sleep in his clothes and hadn't taken a shower yet.

"Make sure you eat, Bella went to buy you some food, we heard you liked Subway."

*Now, where could they have possibly heard that?* "Damien!" Grace exclaimed out loud.

"Don't be upset with him sweetie, it's just who he is, it's what he does. Don't take it personal." Feeling like an overfilled balloon ready to burst into pieces, Grace had had it, she could no longer contain herself. She was sleep-deprived and in pain, her first boyfriend had betrayed her, she was tired of hearing clients come in and out of that house to defile those girls.

"Don't take it personal?" Grace asked with a sarcastically baffled expression on her face, as she began to laugh. "I've been sitting here tied to a pipe for hours. I was drugged, kidnapped, and taken to a sex house by my boyfriend, who I trusted. Y'all are making money off sick people who don't care about destroying these girl's lives, and these poor girls have issues of their own. Apparently, y'all don't care about destroying their lives either. I've never seen so much evil in my life. Well, I take that back. Y'all are just like the terrorists who killed my dad. Selfish and prideful. You think y'all got this amazing money-making business going for y'all, please! Believe it or not, you have to answer to God. Forget the court, forget jail, forget the police, y'all have to answer to God! And if you refuse to get it together, it's going to be super hot where you'll be going, and you can't take that little raggedy fire extinguisher with you." Grace furiously screamed as she pointed to a fire extinguisher sitting in the corner of the room, on top of a box of trash. "Bernice told me that after today, my life would never be the same, but I have a feeling that after today, your life won't ever be the same either," Grace continued as she smiled. "You thought you were just conducting business as usual. Unfortunately for you, I'm unusual." Grace didn't know where this was coming from, she just knew she'd had it, and Rolo needed to hear about Jesus, just as much as everyone else. Then she remembered Matthew 10:19, *But when they arrest you, do not worry about what to say or how to say it. At that time you will be given what to say.* "Y'all intended to harm me, to use me, to break me, but God will get the glory in this!" She continued. "Yo,I got Jesus in my corner."

Rolo stared at Grace in silence for a long minute with the most devious, sadistic, smile she'd ever seen. "First of all, your god stories of doom and gloom, they don't scare me. That religion stuff is for the weak minded, misguided, and uninformed. All of which I am not. Secondly, you call it evil, I call it business. What is the difference from what we are doing than what they're doing in Vegas? It's all business. It just hasn't made its way to being legal here in Maryland yet. If they've already made it legal in one state, that tells you that it's legitimate, and everyone just hasn't gotten on board yet," Rolo explained.

"So, because it's legal, means it's cool?" Grace asked Rolo. He ignored her question and continued with his explanation.

"I wasn't finished talking. Don't interrupt me again, and don't forget where you are." His threats didn't faze Grace at all. She was full of the fire of God at this point, and she could literally feel the Holy Spirit around her. She knew that as a

Christian, her battle had always been against the spirit. Rolo was just a result of whatever she was dealing with in the spirit. Grace knew she just had to continue trusting God.

"Anyway, as I was saying, the public accepts rules when it's legal, period. And they stone stuff that isn't legal. When it's not legal, it automatically tells the weak human mind that its evil," Rolo explained. "Think about it, before Roe versus Wade, how many people do you think agreed with abortion? I doubt that it was seven out of ten people in America, like it is now. Yeah, I know my statistics. That shows you that people are swayed by what is legal. Although they were still performing their own abortions. You know, those back-alley ones, before that bill was passed. You think what we are doing is new? People been selling their bodies for sex for thousands of years. The system just ain't caught on yet. It's the oldest profession in the world." Dude, it's no such thing as prostitution of minors!" Grace fired back. Confused at Rolo's attempt to justify his line of work, Grace was no closer to being convinced than she was before he began talking. "Oh yeah, and who in the world is Bernice?" Rolo asked, with a baffled look on his face.

Grace's response was interrupted by a yell from downstairs.

"Rolo!" It was Damien, and his shouts seemed to be getting closer. "Rolo!" Damien was now heading into the room with Grace and Rolo.

"Bro, it better be some kind of emergency for you to be yelling my name like that." Damien had so much anxiety and guilt.

"Oh," Damien responded with relief as he made eye contact with Grace, realizing she was still chained up in the introduction room. "My bad, bro, have you seen Leon? That dude still got my car," Damien said, not wanting to alert Rolo about his true intentions.

"Nah, I ain't seen him, but let me talk to you for a minute," Rolo said, grabbing Damien's shoulder to lead him into the hallway. He closed the door behind them. "Aye, I talked to Leon right before I texted you about Grace's upcoming client list this evening. He told me he was out lining up clients for her and he'd be back this evening."

Damien didn't say anything. *Dude is a straight liar! That's why he wasn't answering his phone, he was lying about it being dead.* Damien thought angrily to himself. He felt so stupid, he fell for Leon's scheme. *But if he lied about that, he must've thought that it was going to bother me, which means there's no telling what else he may be scheming on.* Damien knew from that moment on he had to watch his back. If Leon was keeping the fact that he was lining up clients for Grace from Damien, it must mean only one thing: He felt Damien was getting soft and was too involved with Grace. If that was the case, it was just a matter of time before Leon and Rolo fully turned against him. He was now a liability, a loose end. It was now 2 p.m., and evening was such a vague time frame. He didn't know if they meant six in the evening or nine in the evening.

All Damien knew was that he needed to get both himself and Grace out of that house as soon as he could. He didn't have his car, so if they did get out of the house successfully, he would have to take Rolo's sports car to get away. He didn't know where Rolo kept his keys, so that became the first thing on his to-do list, to find Rolo's keys, so he and Grace could have a speedy escape.

"Oh, okay, cool. Well let me try to hit him up again, this dude is riding around with all of my money, I forgot to take it out before he left this morning," Damien said as he turned to walk away. Rolo turned and went back into the room with Grace, closing the door behind him. Damien headed straight for Rolo's room to find the car keys and a gun. Not only had he left his cash in his car the night before, he'd also left his gun in the glove compartment. Damien moved quickly down the hall to Rolo's room. The door was already open, so he walked to his nightstand. Right on top was something shiny, Rolos' favorite gun, the one he called Keisha: a silver 357 Magnum. Damien picked it up and opened the chamber, making sure it was loaded. Not fully loaded, but more than enough bullets, at least that's what he hoped. He then opened the nightstand drawer and, surprisingly, the car keys were right there, the only thing in the drawer. *That was easier than I thought. Too easy*, he thought. *It may be too good to be true.* Knowing how complicated and detailed Rolo was, Damien had expected the keys and gun to be in a secret safe, guarded by impenetrable metal and a retinal scan. With time not on his side, Damien tucked the gun away in the back of his belt, making sure his jacket covered it up.

As he tucked the gun away, he heard a loud scream followed by "Get off me!" *Grace! Rolo is alone with her!* He dashed out of the room and down the hall to her rescue.

He sprinted down the hallway with tunnel vision, seeing nothing but getting Grace out of that house, as soon as he could. He needed to get to Grace quickly, before her life was ruined. As Damien threw open the door to the introduction room, his fears were confirmed. Rolo stood over Grace, trying to secure both of her arms to the pipe. *It'll be easier for him to rape her*, he thought. *Without her arms, she'd be even more defenseless.* Grace was fighting back, flailing all over the place, there wasn't a part of her body that wasn't moving. Damien was happy to see he'd made it in time. Not thinking twice, Damien pulled the gun from the back of his pants and aimed it directly at Rolo. Hands shaking and sweat beading up on his face, Damien was ready to pull the trigger. He'd never shot anyone before, and in this moment, he didn't want to shoot Rolo either, but he was prepared to.

"Get up, leave her alone, and step over there," Damien exclaimed, using the gun to point to the left of the room. With a bewildered expression, Rolo made eye contact with Damien, stood up slowly, then smirked.

"Three years Damien, you gon abandon three years for this chic?!" Rolo asked, changing his smirk to a serious demeanor.

"I said go stand over there, Rolo." Damien pointed the gun at the wall to his left, ignoring his words. Rolo backed away, staring at Damien.

"Now turn around and face the wall."

"Bro, what is this, timeout?" Rolo asks jokingly.

"Just turn around Rolo." Despite his state of nervousness, Damien sounded calm.

Rolo threw up his hands in surrender and turned around. "Okay, whatever you say."

Damien quickly made his way over to a partially unrestrained Grace, since Rolo hadn't been able to cuff her other arm to the pipe. Grace stared at Damien, with a mixture of contempt and confusion in her eyes. "We gettin' outta here, alright." Damien assures her.

Grace doesn't respond, but continued to stare at Damien. *What is happening? Is he going to try to rape me too? Am I hallucinating because I haven't eaten? Am I delirious?* Grace didn't know how to respond to Damien, how to think about him, or what to think about him. There was a lot going on in that moment.

"Aye Rolo, throw me the keys, I know you got 'em." Damien exclaimed to Rolo, kneeling next to Grace. Rolo complied without a fight, reaching into his back pocket and tossing them to Damien. Grace was still speechless, she'd thought Rolo was going to succeed at stealing her virginity. Although she was putting up a fight, for a few seconds she had lost hope. When Rolo walked back into the room after his talk with Damien, the expression on his face said everything. He didn't even need to open his mouth. The expression was evil, it was suggestive, it was indicative of the very thing Grace had feared. She knew right away that she had to fight. When he tried to secure both of her hands to the pipe, she immediately began screaming and fighting, throwing her body around to prevent his plan from succeeding. She wasn't sure how long she'd been fighting with Rolo, it'd felt like forever, but it wasn't that long before Damien interrupted Rolo. The very person who was responsible for her being there was now the one attempting to rescue her. She didn't know whether to be angry and disgusted, or grateful to Damien. Or both. Damien picked up the keys and, before uncuffing Grace, their eyes met. It was only for a second, but it was enough time for Grace to see the regret and remorse in his eyes. Her dad always told her that folk's eyes told a story. He'd say, "there go those eyes, talking to me." He could read her like a book, and she didn't realize how until she got a little older. She began paying attention to people's eyes. She noticed how expressive they were. When she and Damien looked at each other, she had a flashback of her dad looking at her with those big brown eyes, and that smile that could light up a room. She had an Ernest moment.

Damien's eyes said everything. She wanted to be angry with him, but felt her anger and hostility melting away. She actually felt sorry for him. *Whatever possessed him to lead this life for years had to be more of a burden that what I experienced these last few hours*, she thought. As the handcuffs fell to the floor, Grace was free again. Damien reached his hand to help Grace off the floor. Reluctantly, she took his hand and stood up. Looking down at her wrists, she realized indentations from the handcuff marked her right wrist. Caressing her wrist, Grace realized she was still dressed in the clothing she'd had on in the photo shoot, except she was barefoot.

"We gotta go, Grace. We can worry about that later." Seeing the look on her face, Damien turned to Rolo, making sure he was still facing the wall and nudged Grace's shoulder, encouraging her to pick up the pace.

With Rolo's keys in hand, Damien and Grace rushed to the door, down the hallway, then, down the stairs to the front door. As they opened the door, they were standing face to face with Leon, front door key in hand, he was trying to open the door. Behind him were two men.

# Chapter 11

Giving no time for Leon to react, Damien pulled out his gun, aimed it toward Leon and the two men, and ordered them into the house. Grace was terrified. She felt how cruel and sadistic Leon seemed at the festival, and she didn't know how this was going to play out. She had a horrible feeling in her gut. Leon smirked, then looked from Damien to Grace. He did not move. The other two men, visibly terrified, hastily entered the house. They moved so fast they ran into Grace, almost knocking her to the ground.

"Shoot him, Leon!" a loud voice shouted from upstairs. It was Rolo. Damien grabbed Grace's hand, and together, they ran outside, past Leon to Rolo's car. As they ran, Grace looked back and saw that Leon had a small handgun aimed at her and Damien.

"Damien!" Grace yelled frantically, pushing Damien to the ground, away from Leon's gun. The gun fired, and was followed up by the sound of impact. Shaken from the dive to the ground, Damien managed to see what was hit. His Mustang. The bullet hit the driver's door of his Mustang. Realizing that Leon probably wouldn't stop firing until they both were dead, Damien, still on the ground, pulled Rolo's gun from the back of his pants, aimed it at Leon, and fired.

Leon dropped the gun, grabbed his stomach, and fell to his knees. Damien, in shock at what just happened, grabbed Grace's hand and led her down the driveway to Rolo's car.

"Oh my God, oh my God, oh my God! Damien! Is he going to die?" Grace asked, horrified, as they ran for the car.

"I hope not, I'll call 9–1–1 once we're in the car."

Grace's mind and heart were racing, and she felt like she was in a dream. She couldn't believe she'd just been shot at and someone had actually attempted to kill her and Damien. Damien was visibly shaken but didn't deviate from his escape plan. He knew that if he stayed to help Leon, Rolo would soon be at the door, possibly with a gun to finish what Leon started.

As they neared the car, Damien unlocked the doors with the automatic key. The noise sounded like freedom to Grace. They were really leaving that awful house! As they climbed into the vehicle, they quickly shared a glance, both felt relief that they had escaped Leon's gunfire, but were worried about what would happen to him. Neither wanted him to die. As he backed down the driveway, Damien took one last look at the scene near the front door. Rolo was running toward Leon. Damien skidded down the driveway, into the street. He had completed his mission of saving Grace but failed in his desire to never use a gun. Damien feared guns. After Mr. Wright and Tyrell's deaths from gun violence, Damien didn't want anything to do with guns. He knew he needed to have one for safety, especially in his line of work, but he had hoped to never actually use it.

"Yes, I'd like to report a shooting. Someone was shot at 3131 Fettyville Way. Please just send someone over there, he's been shot in the stomach." Damien frantically reported to the 9–1–1 operator on the other end.

"Sir, can you tell me your name?" the 9–1–1 operator asked gently.

"Sorry ma'am, can you just send someone?" Damien responded, ending the call, then carelessly dropping his phone into the cup holder. Grace and Damien were now down the street from Hotel Rolo. Grace felt she was in a live action scene from a horror movie. She saw only one other house at the very end of the road. *They picked a perfect spot to run their unlawful business out of, no neighbors, no one around to pick up on the suspicious activity*, she thought. A chill ran down Grace's body. Her adrenaline was crashing and she realized she was freezing. She was finally beginning to calm down and believed that they really had escaped. Noticing her discomfort, Damien turned the car's heater to eighty degrees. The red sports car had leather seats, which didn't help the cold at all.

"Thank you," Grace said with reluctant gratitude, still conflicted about Damien and his role in her abduction.

"Nah, thank you. You could have left me hanging, and just looked out for yourself back there. Which would've been understandable, considering, you know," Damien said, shamefaced. He couldn't believe what he had turned into, Aunt Mildred, Mr. Wright, and Tyrell would be so disappointed. He didn't even want to discuss his role, who he'd become, the shame was overwhelming. All those girls' lives he'd helped to destroy. The memories of what he had done began filling his mind, he felt like he couldn't focus or breathe, he was losing his grip. His heart had never beat so fast. He didn't know what was moving faster, his thoughts or his heart. Suddenly, he slammed on the brakes and put the car in park, right in the middle of the road. He then balled up his fists and began to punch the steering wheel, over and over again. Tears began to flow from his eyes. Grace was floored by his outburst and did not know whether to console him or get out of the car and run. Then she knew. The soft whisper of the Holy Spirit said "Mourn with those who mourn." It clicked. This man was mourning. Mourning all the mistakes he'd made, and probably the fact that he just shot and potentially killed his friend. Seeing Damien cry brought back a memory of her dad crying, as he poured his heart out to God, one Sunday in church.

He had just gotten back from his first tour in Iraq and he was mourning the loss of two good friends from his unit. He blamed himself for their deaths, for reasons that were never discussed with Grace. She was curious, but she never asked him about it. Since he didn't bring up the details, she thought it was best to leave it alone. After church that day, Ernest told Grace that God had told him to let it go, that it wasn't his fault, and if he didn't allow God to deal with that pain and guilt he was harboring, the pain would continue to deal with him.

After Damien was through with his outburst, Grace waited a few seconds, then asked Damien to move the car from the middle of the road. Pointing to an area on the right side of the street, she asked, "You mind if we move over there? I just don't want us, you know, getting smashed up."

Grace couldn't resist an opportunity to throw a joke in there, as she was hoping it would lighten Damien's mood, just a little. They weren't on a busy street; however, they were right in the middle of it, and Grace didn't want a car or a semi running into them. He kept quiet but eased the car off the road and even managed to crack a smirk.

They were in the middle of nowhere, surrounded by farmland and fallen red and brown leaves. Grace looked over at Damien, tears still spilling from his eyes. Giving him a moment, not wanting to rush him or ruin his moment of release, she gently placed her hand on his shoulder, silently reassuring him that things were going to be okay, in spite of everything.

After about ten minutes of tears, Damien still hadn't spoken a word. He was staring at the floor of the car. Growing impatient and uncomfortable with Damien's silence and blank stare, Grace interrupted.

"Damien! Snap out of it, bro," she exclaimed. She didn't know what was going on with him. Startled by the interruption, Damien jumped, then looked over at Grace. His eyes were so puffy and red, he was almost unrecognizable. His swollen eyes startled Grace, but she didn't flinch. She maintained her composure, despite the almost unrecognizable man sitting next to her. "You good?"

"All these years I spent running away. Running away from pain, from trauma, from who I knew I was supposed to be. Man, I'm tired, I feel like it's eating away at my soul, if I even have one of those left."

Feeling sorry for Damien, Grace paused to think, taking a deep breath. "Yep, you still have a soul; you need to stop playing all of that Mortal Kombat."

Her joke forces a surprised chuckle out of Damien. "How do you do that? I mean, after everything I did to you, everything you been through in less than one day, you still manage to crack jokes. Like, c'mon, how are you not trying to shoot me, call the cops on me, I don't know, something other than sitting in this car with me cracking corny jokes?"

"Well, that's a legit question, when I first realized you were responsible for this, I wanted to. I wanted you to suffer, just like you caused all of those other girls to suffer, but God showed me that you were already hurting. I didn't know why, but He reminded me that people who are hurting often times end up hurting other people, and I was reminded of the mercy He'd shown me. So, since I don't really know the real Damien, why don't you tell me about the real you?"

Damien immediately felt overwhelmed. He had been someone else for so long, the thought of explaining who he really was, his true history, felt pretty daunting. But he was also tired, tired of being this imposter, tired of using other people to run from his pain, tired of playing a tough guy who didn't have a soul, tired of destroying girls' lives, but most of all, he was tired of running from the God he knew had been there all along. He knew all of those scriptures he kept seeing weren't a coincidence, although he wanted to believe they were. He was comfortable not dealing with his issues. Tyrell got it; he didn't allow their previous life circumstances to define his life and his future, Tyrell didn't allow the fact that his mom and dad literally packed up and left him at home one day ruin his life and keep him from God. His parents never came back for him. He was tired of carrying the pain from Mr. Wright and Tyrell's death alone. He was tired of destroying himself. He was tired of being selfish. Tired of causing other's pain. It was easier to hide from God than to allow God to help him. It was easy to live the lie, because the truth required Damien to face his pain. It required Damien to surrender to God and to begin leaning on Him.

All of the running was exhausting, but until he met Grace, he didn't realize just how exhausted he really was. He didn't realize that out of all the girls he had met and used in the past, she would be the one that ended his "career." Sitting in the car with her, however, brought on the realization that he actually had deep feelings for her. It felt strange to him. He'd hadn't felt something so passionate for someone since Mr. Wright, Tyrell, and Aunt Mildred.

"The real me?" Damien asked after a couple minutes of silence.

"Yes, please. The real you," Grace responded with a bright smile, still processing the trauma she just endured, she tried hard to put on a brave front. Although she still felt sick and severely hurt on the inside.

"Well, let's see." Damien took another deep breath, not excited about how Grace could respond to the real him, since she apparently fell for the impostor. "That may be a lot to digest, you sure you want to know me for real?"

"Yes, Damien, I'm sure. You think this is my first rodeo with an impostor? Please, serving in ministry and outreach I've seen my fair share of people pretending to be someone they're not."

"Alright then. Well, for starters, I don't go to Howard, I never even finished high school." Damien stopped and looked at Grace, waiting for a reaction. Her expression was blank and unfazed, waiting for him to continue his story as if he didn't just reveal a huge lie.

Damien turned back to face the steering wheel, he didn't want to have this conversation while looking in Grace's eyes, as there was so much guilt, shame, and pain related to his story. "I know I told you that I was from New Jersey, and that's where my parents live/ Truth is, I am from here, and when I was three years old, my dad shot and killed my mom, then killed himself." Grace's stomach dropped to her feet. "None of my family wanted to take me in, some of them actually blamed me for what my dad did, for reasons I still don't understand seventeen years later. I mean, how could a three-year-old old cause a grown man to kill the mother of his son, his wife?! My great aunt Mildred was the only one who wanted to adopt me, but the state prevented her from being able to, since she had a mental illness. They said she was unfit to care for me. So, I ended up in several group and foster homes. She'd come see me and pick me up from time to time, and that was comforting. It helped take my mind off the orphan life for those moments I was able to spend with her. She always boasted on how intelligent I was and how she wanted me to go to Howard once I graduated."

"So that's where the inspiration for the Howard cover came about," Grace interrupted.

"Yep. Sort of, I will get to that in a minute. When I was fifteen, she passed away from lung cancer. After that, I lost a huge part of me. I lost motivation to finish school because Howard was her dream for me. Since she was no longer alive to see me achieve it, it was no longer a motivation for me. Shortly after she died, me and two of my friends from the group home, Tyrell and Josiah, ran away. We were living on the streets for only a couple of days before this barber, Mr. Wright..."

"Wait! You aren't talking about Mr. Mufasa Wright, are you?" Grace asked excitedly.

"Yep, you knew him?"

"I did. He and my dad were good acquaintances, and that was his go-to barber. Small world!" Grace replied.

"True, that's crazy, yo. I wonder if we ever crossed paths before July? Well, Mr. Wright found us sleeping in front of his shop one day. Guess he felt sorry for us, he ended up giving us all under-the-table jobs, then a few months later, he adopted all three of us. All three of us, yo! Who does that? We couldn't believe it;

someone actually wanted to adopt not one, but three teenaged boys."

Grace was filled with questions, but she didn't want to keep interrupting Damien, as she imagined this was the first time in a long time that he'd talked about the real Damien. She waited patiently for the right time for her questions.

"About a year later, at the end of my junior year in high school, Tyrell and Mr. Wright were killed." Damien paused, visibly and audibly fighting back tears. Again, Grace put her hand on Damien's shoulder. "Now that right there, that broke me," Damien explained. "It hit harder than Aunt Mildred dying. Maybe because I knew she was sick? I don't know. I just know that I didn't understand it. How could these Christians who loved God so much be killed? Like why didn't it happen to Josiah or me? Man, we rejected them so hard. We made fun of them, and they were the real ones. They weren't afraid to be vulnerable, to die, to be sold out to what they believed. They were constantly talking about Jesus, the Bible, salvation, the Holy Spirit, church, changing lives... And they had so much joy. So much life ... passion ... vision. So much hope. So much promise ..." Damien stopped and took another long break.

Grace took this opportunity to interject since she wouldn't be cutting him off. "Can I say something to that?"

"To what?" Damien asked.

"To what you said about your family being killed?"

"Oh yeah, go ahead," Damien said.

Grace took another deep breath. "You know when my dad died, I did not want to have anything to do with God. I seriously thought He was punishing us for something. I thought He'd abandoned us. I couldn't understand why our protector didn't protect us. My heart went numb when I found out my dad had died. But through constant love and patience from my mom, she helped me to realize that God is still God, and that while we tend to treat death as a punishment, for believers it's the beginning of their amazing new life with Jesus. That truth eventually gave me peace and reconciled me back to God. My dad, man he left an amazing legacy. The impact he made on my mother and I, and others, is still holding weight, and his life is still drawing people to Christ. I don't understand everything God does and allows, but I trust Him, completely. When you think about Mr. Wright and Tyrell, think about how joyful and problem-free they are. Also, if that had been you or Josiah, unfortunately, I wouldn't be able to say the same about y'all's destination. So, have peace in that truth, Damien. Be grateful for the time you got to spend with them, be grateful for their lives and their legacy, and if you desire, keep their legacy going."

"Man, all of that sounds great and everything, but I sincerely feel like it's too late. I'm tired of this life, of this façade, but what kind of good life could actually be in store for me? I mean, I'm probably going to be facing at least five years in jail, I messed up so many lives, I almost destroyed the life of the only girl I ever..." Damien stopped mid-sentence. "I mean, what kind of life is in my future?"

Floored by Damien's partial admission, Grace thought, *He loves me? Nah, maybe he was going to say cared for, or liked, or dated.*" She almost dismissed his admission of hopelessness because she was so confused by his near admission. "Damien, the fact that you and I are sitting in this car right now is proof that there is hope for you. Dude, you're still alive. And I know you're feeling God tugging at your heart, I can hear it when you speak. He didn't die for you, just for you to have a life of no value. And the stuff you did can be forgiven. Paul destroyed people's lives, too. He killed Christians. But this man turned out to be one of the greatest people in the Bible. God saw him Damien, He chose him, in spite of what he did, He chose him. His love is that great. But you, you have to be willing to not just accept Jesus into your heart, but also allow Him to take that guilt off your shoulders and put it upon His shoulders. You can't walk around with the weight of your past sins your entire life, it will destroy you and keep you from experiencing the life God desires for you. But you have to want to be free. You have to want it badly enough for yourself, Damien."

Damien sat in silence for a few minutes, fiddling with the steering wheel, and digesting all of the good news Grace had just expressed to him. He finally broke the silence with a slight chuckle. "You know, you remind me so much of them. This conversation is bringing back so many memories of the annoying conversations I had with them back in the day. Back then, it was annoying, but what I wouldn't give to have those conversations with them again. I was so young and stubborn." Damien took another deep breath and closed his eyes for what seemed like an entire minute. "Alright, what I gotta do?"

"What do you gotta do for what?" Grace asked, not understanding Damien's question.

"I mean, what do I need to do to get Christian?" Not wanting to discourage Damien, Grace kept her chuckles about Damien's desire to "get Christian" to herself. Instead, she smiled, excited at his request. Anytime someone gave their life to Christ, it put Grace on cloud nine. Despite everything Damien had done to her and others, Grace forgave him. She learned a long time ago that forgiveness was a necessary part of her life, and the life of a Christian period. She wasn't going to allow hate and an unwillingness to forgive enslave her or prevent her own forgiveness.

"Well, it's really simple, just repeat after me, and be one hundred percent sincere. If you don't agree with my words, you can change them to fit what's in your heart. It just needs to be sincere. First, we confess our sins, then we acknowledge that Jesus is Lord and Savior, then we ask Him to come into our hearts and forgive us. Okay, here we go. Jesus, I know I am a sinner."

"Jesus, I know I am a sinner."

"I believe you are Lord and Savior."

"I believe you are Lord and Savior."

"Please come into my heart and forgive me of my sins. Thank you, Jesus for saving me!"

"Please come into my heart and forgive me of my sins. Thank you, Jesus, for saving me!"

Eyes closed; Damien repeated every word. After they were done, Damien remained in silence for about five minutes. Tears ran down his face once again, but this time the tears represented something different. They weren't tears of shame and guilt, they were tears of restoration, freedom, redemption, and forgiveness.

"How do you feel?" Grace asked.

"Yo, like a 300-pound weight lifted off my shoulders." Damien exclaimed with excitement.

Grace smiled even brighter than before. And shouted a very loud "Wooohooo!! Bro, this is the most important day of your life, praise God!! I'm so happy for you."

"Appreciate it, Grace. Thanks for being you, despite me, despite everything."

Grace smiled.

"So, what now?" Damien asked.

"Well, the journey has begun. From this day forward, you're a new man. God has given you a new identity. Now, your whooollleeeee life's mission has changed, now you live to please Him, to love Him, and to show other people how to love Him," Grace explained with great enthusiasm and a huge smile. "I will have time to explain more once we get out of here, but right now, we have to get back to my house. I know my mom is probably losing her mind. First, we need to let the police know what's going down in that house. I gotta help Bernice and those other girls, but I don't think we should try to play heroes, we should let the cops handle it."

With racing thoughts running through Damien's head, he felt excited for his new journey with God, but fearful as well, knowing that it was a possibility that prison was in his near future. "Okay, I should probably make that call, but who is Bernice?" he asked.

"Why are you the second person to ask me that very same question today? Rolo asked me the same thing when I mentioned her. Maybe she goes by another name or something? She is one of the Hispanic girls."

Confused, Damien squinted his eyes and tilted his head, trying to think of who Grace was referring to. "There is only one

Hispanic girl in that house, and her name is Latrice," he explained.

Now feeling confused herself, Grace recalled the conversations she had with Bernice and how encouraging she was. She even talked about God once or twice but did seem to avoid giving details about her life. Grace did a lot of the talking, but the few words that Bernice did get across were very encouraging to Grace. Now, wondering if she was hallucinating from Leon drugging her the night before, or from lack of sleep, Grace was concerned.

"What in the world?" Grace asks, confusedly. "You're playing with me, right? Either I'm losing my mind, or you didn't know there was another Hispanic girl in that house."

"Grace, I am one hundred percent positive there was only one Hispanic girl there. There were five girls in that house, not including Bella. All of them have been there for at least one year, so we know them pretty well. Their real names, their given names, their family, where they're from, what they like and don't like, and so on. We know everything about them. As much as I hate to admit it, it's a huge part of what allowed us to maintain control over them. Knowing that information and being able to use that information at any given time against them if they were to get out of line. I know you were handcuffed when you were brought in, but that's not our thing, we don't have to do that. What we use to keep them bound is all psychological, all mental. Well some physical, Leon and Rolo have been physical when the girls didn't meet quota or got "outta line." But yeah, let me call the police before Rolo leaves Leon to die and tries to set up shop somewhere else." Grabbing his cell phone from the cup holder,

Damien is surprised to feel his hand shaking, almost uncontrollably. Fear was creeping back with a vengeance. He knew reporting what was going on in that house meant confessing his involvement, sooner or later.

"Whatever happens, Damien, God is with you," Grace encouraged him, as she saw his anxiety and reservations about making the call.

"I needed to hear that, thanks Grace. I guess I should prepare myself for whatever consequences I may face huh? Those girls deserve justice."

"That's true, they do, and God is also a God of reconciliation and mercy, so don't count Him out when it comes to this situation. Just do your part, and let God handle everything. If jail is a result, He has your back," Grace reassured him.

Damien had never felt as much peace as he felt in that moment. Hearing "God has your back" was something that actually pertained to him now. It's a truth he could actually reconcile with, considering the fact that he actually knew Jesus now, and he wasn't running away from Him anymore. He felt comfort in knowing that whatever happened, God was going to be with Him.

"9–1–1, what's your emergency?"

Damien took a deep breath. "I wanted to report a crime at 3131 Fettyville Way. There are five underage girls being held there, and one adult female. They all have been reported missing, except for the adult. Their names are Latrice, Tamara, Unique, Malia, Brittany, and the woman's name is Camille. The girls have been sold multiple times for sex out of that house. Bye." Damien ended the call before the operator could ask any more questions, then looked over at Grace, who is giving him a comforting smile.

"After I take you home, I'm turning myself in, as well as giving them information on Rolo and Leon, if he's still alive." Those words caused Damien's stomach to drop. "Maybe we should pray for Leon?" he asked. "You know, that he would survive and not die?"

"Yes! We most definitely should," Grace replied, closing her eyes. Damien immediately imitated her.

"Father, we come to you in Jesus's name asking that you will heal Leon and help him to survive, we also pray that you deal with his heart and save him, in Jesus name, amen."

"Amen," Damien echoed.

"You ready to take me home?" asked Grace.

"Honestly, not really," Damien said. "Yo, this has been one of the most awful, amazing days of my life. I would rather soak in this moment before I go back to reality. But, I gotta get you home." Turning the key in the ignition, Damien put the car in drive and headed to Grace's house.

# Chapter 12

During the thirty-minute drive to her house, Grace could not stop thinking about Bernice. She was certain that all of her interactions with Bernice had indeed taken place. She just couldn't believe that the entire night with her was a hallucination. Since Damien had just given his life to Jesus, shot his friend, and was on his way to turning himself into the police, she didn't want to bring it up again. Grace didn't want to add extra hysteria to his plate, or scare him, have him thinking Christianity consisted of weird people with imaginary friends. Plus, the look he gave her when she insisted that Bernice was real was all she needed to leave that situation alone. She just couldn't shake her experience or get Bernice out of her mind. *Her beautiful face, and her mysterious past, who in the world was Bernice?*

"Damien!" Grace yelled abruptly as they both turned their attention to a young woman standing in the middle of the street. Damien slammed on his brakes, as they were about twenty feet away from the young woman. As they came to a screeching halt, the woman hurriedly ran to the curb. They stopped just a few feet from where she was standing.

"Oh my goodness, thank you, God! Dude, we just almost hit that girl! This cannot be good!" Grace exclaimed. "What in the world is wrong with her, why was she just standing in the middle of the street?!" Angry, with her anxiety levels up again, Grace didn't even realize they were on her street, and right in front of her house. She had been in a daze for the entire ride, thinking about Bernice, and how that experience couldn't have been her imagination. She was actually beginning to think she may have been losing her mind a little. It just didn't make sense.

"Bernice!?" Grace asks as she stares at the young woman they had almost hit. She stared back at them.

"Oh man, I see you're trippin' again," Damien said as he followed Grace's stare to the girl on the street.

"Dude, that looks just like her, no, that is her! But in different clothes? Why is she in front of my house? Wait, how'd she get out of the house?! How does she know where I live?! Aye, I feel like I'm in the twilight zone or something."

"Wait, hold up, I do know her, but not from the house," Damien said. "I think I may have gone to high school with her. Yoooooo! I did. She hung around Tyrell from time to time, during our track practices. She was cool, but she didn't talk much. This is the girl you said was at the house? We should probably get out of the car, huh?"

"Man, I ain't budging, this girl was just standing in the middle of the street like something straight out of a horror movie, now she's just standing there staring at us. Something is not right, Damien. I already feel like I'm starting to lose it." Grace's words are abruptly cut short when she sees her mother.

Tasha was walking, with the aid of her crutches, down the stairs, sheer joy on her face. It was an expression she had seen on her mother in the past. During her dad's first deployment, Tasha and Grace had gone several weeks without hearing from him. On the twenty-third day of not receiving any communication from Ernest, he finally video called them. It was one of the best days of their lives. To see him alive and smiling from the desert was an answer to their prayers. The worry was over, the fear that something terrible happened to him was over, and they were once again reunited, even if it was just a virtual reunion. As Grace refocused her attention to the present, she sees her mother's face. Tears streamed from her eyes down her high cheekbones, and she had a gigantic smile on her face. Grace knew exactly what that expression said.

"Grace!!" Tasha yelled as she made her way to greet her daughter, who finally got out of the car and ran to greet her mother. Tasha dropped the crutches at the bottom of the stairs, and her arms were outstretched for an emotional welcome hug. Grace couldn't believe she was actually looking at her mom in the flesh. She felt like a little girl, so excited to reunite with Tasha and tell her everything. After the night she had endured, she didn't know when she would actually see her mother again. During her moments of hopelessness, she didn't know *if* she would even see her again.

The enemy really had done a job on her faith the previous night. Seeing all of those girls in that house, listening to Bernice tell her about each one of them, made Grace's escape from that place seem impossible. All the girls in that house were runaways, abandoned in some way, or lured there with promises of shelter, food, security, and love. With them on her mind, it made the reunion with her mom that much more meaningful. She was grateful.

Grace finally reached her mother's arms! She was careful not to run into her with too much force, since Tasha dropped her crutches on the ground. Grace didn't want their reunion to end with Tasha going to the hospital. Grace's eyes welled up with tears.

"Ma, oh my God, you have no idea, I missed you so much!" Grace sobbed as the tears began to flow uncontrollably down her face.

"I know Grace Face, I know, I missed you like crazy!" Tasha replied, tears also flowing down her face.

"I have so much to tell you, Ma." Grace and Tasha didn't want to let go of each other. The hug felt like it lasted for five minutes.

"I know, but first, can you grab my crutches and tell Damien to come here so we can all talk?"

Grace knew the trouble Damien was facing and the fear he was experiencing because of it, and she knew that confessing to her mom was one of the last things he wanted to do.

Grace picked up the crutches and handed them to her mom. As she turned to walk back to the car to get Damien, she noticed Bernice was gone. "Wait a minute, did you see that girl that was standing on the curb? We almost hit her when we were pulling up?" Grace asked her mom.

"Yep, I saw her; I was actually talking to her right before y'all got here. But go get Damien, I will tell you the rest when we get out of this cold and sit down."

Perplexed, Grace wondered what in the world Bernice could have been telling her mom. *Who is Bernice, really? What was she doing at my house? How did she get out of that house? Where are the other girls? Why hasn't mom asked where I've been?* Grace wondered.

"Okay." Grace replied and walked back toward the car.

Trying to read Grace's expression, Damien stared intently at her as she walked up to the driver's side window. As she approached the car, Damien began to let the window down.

"Hey, you can pull up a little closer to the house if you want. My mom wants to talk to both of us."

"O-kay," Damien responded reluctantly. He knew he'd have to face Tasha eventually and deal with her emotions after she found out about his involvement in her daughter's disappearance. Anxious at the thought of that confession and conversation, Damien sat in the driver seat for another minute. He felt paralyzed. The thoughts of what he did, not just to Grace, but to Tasha as well, were coming back full force, and the thought of confessing that to Tasha frightened him. Grace didn't know what he and Leon had done to Tasha the night before. He felt more afraid in that moment than he did when Leon was shooting at them.

"Damien!" Grace called, interrupting Damien's thoughts. "Don't trip so much, I got ya back." She assured him, with that captivating smile that Damien loved to see. Smiling back at her, and feeling a little more at peace, Damien pulled the car forward a few more feet to park directly in front of Tasha's house. As he got out of the car, he realized that the girl he'd almost hit was no longer there. Perplexed, he turned to Grace, who had been waiting for him to park so they could walk into the house together.

"Yo, What the heck? Grace where'd that girl go? Did you see her leave?" Damien asked. Grace didn't say anything, she just gave Damien a perplexed look, shook her head, and shrugged.

## Chapter 13

"I'm going to change these ridiculous clothes really quickly. I'll be back," Grace said to Tasha and Damien, who were sitting in the living room. Damien sat uncomfortably on the brown leather couch, but not because the couch was uncomfortable. Damien felt as though he was in a courtroom, and Tasha was both the prosecutor and the judge. He refused to look up, or even in her direction, as she sat right across from him. He picked with his nails, cracked his knuckles, and fixed his shoelaces, anything he could do to avoid making eye contact with Tasha. The minutes it took Grace to change felt like years to Damien. He and Tasha sat in complete silence for those two minutes. He had never felt his hands sweating so profusely.

When Grace walked back into the living room in her grey sweatpants and matching Balentine High sweatshirt, Damien was relieved. Taking a seat a couple feet away from Damien on the couch, Grace could not believe she was at home, sitting on her couch, looking at her mother. That experience, although it didn't last long at all, was highly traumatic, and being back home so soon, she knew it was God's hand.

"You're comfortable now?" Tasha asked Grace.

"Yes, ma'am," Grace replied. There were a few seconds of awkwardness as Tasha gathered her thoughts. Damien and Grace both had a million anxious thoughts running through their minds, and Tasha's demeanor wasn't helping the situation at all. Pulling her hair behind her ears, Tasha finally broke the silence.

"I had a very emotionally overwhelming, depressing, amazing day. First, I woke up this morning with the most excruciating headache I'd ever had. Couldn't understand why my head was hurting so badly, I almost went to the ER, but I was able to get rid of it with some good ole ibuprofen I found in the medicine cabinet." Damien began to rub his hair nervously. Grace quickly caught a glimpse of his nerves following her mom's statement. *Hmm, what could he possibly have to do with Mom's headache?* She wondered, then dismissed it, deciding it would be better to think about it later so she could focus on her mom's story.

"I was expecting to eat some breakfast burritos with my daughter, then maybe head downtown to do some shopping," Tasha explained. "When I realized you hadn't returned, I immediately felt that something was just not right. I tried calling you multiple times, and your phone was going straight to voicemail. Then I called Imani, and she told me that you two were texting last night, and then you'd just stopped texting her. She told me she tried to call you after about an hour of not hearing anything back, and your phone was going straight to voicemail. That conversation had my wheels turning. I began to wonder if you'd even came home last night. Then I went to look in the freezer and fridge, come to find out, we had everything we needed for burritos. Then I remembered that last weekend, we bought a ridiculous amount of ingredients and had enough for the next few weekends. So, I decided to call the police to file a missing person's report. The receptionist told me I needed to wait forty-eight hours to file an official missing person's report but assured me that the police were going to be actively looking for you anyway.

"Now you know me, Grace, you can imagine how I was feeling. I was extremely angry, I could have gone all crazy mama bear on that receptionist. However, I was grateful they were still going to be working to help find you. What's funny is when she transferred me to a cop, he told me that the receptionist was new and still learning the ropes. She misinformed me about the criteria to file a missing person's report. Anyway, long story short, I was able to file one."

Grace and Damien were listening to Tasha tell her story, but they didn't understand why she hadn't asked Grace where she was or what happened. *How much did that Bernice girl tell her?* Grace wondered. *And if she did tell her everything, why is Damien still here and not being hauled off to jail?* Damien and Grace kept sharing quick glances. They both knew what the other was thinking. *What is this story leading to?"*

"What was so frustrating was that I couldn't even give them a description of what you were wearing, because I hadn't seen you this morning. I had to describe to them what you wore last night," Tasha continued, interrupting Grace's thoughts. She let out a deep sigh as she continued. Her tone was mellow, and her expression only slightly distressed. Reliving the events of the morning was pretty traumatic, and it was visibly showing.

"My yellow sweater, your favorite distressed light blue jeans, and brown ankle boots with a brown leather jacket is what I told them you were wearing. Oh, and your khaki purse with an ugly cat on it, that seems to be eternally attached to your body." Tasha forced a laugh, holding back tears.

Damien, beginning to feel the weight of his crimes, rose up off the couch to leave. "You know what, I don't belong here Ms. Tasha, I'm….."

"Damien," Tasha softly interrupted. "Please, sit down. I'm going somewhere with my story, and you're a part of it.

That's why I wanted to talk to both of y'all." Damien silently reclaimed his place on the couch.

"After I spoke to the first officer on the phone, they sent two more over. I basically retold them the same thing. I did let them know about my suspicions of you, Damien. I told them how I wasn't all that fond of you, but you were beginning to grow on me. And Grace, I told them that it was a possibility that you never even came home last night, instead of leaving this morning, as your text indicated. I couldn't confirm that, but I know my daughter wouldn't go spend money on food without checking to see if we already had the ingredients. Then they asked if I thought you could harm her Damien. My response was 'it's possible for anyone to do anything.' I honestly did have my suspicions after I realized we had the ingredients for the burritos. Things just weren't adding up. I wasn't sure if you killed her or kidnapped her. Or if someone killed you, then kidnapped Grace. Or if someone killed or kidnapped both of y'all. Then I didn't have a number for you, Damien, and I was just kicking myself for that.

"The police were great. They were really compassionate and attentive, I really appreciated that. I didn't feel rushed or shamed, and I didn't feel they were more concerned about other cases. Before they left, they assured me that they were going to do everything they could to find you. I couldn't walk, I didn't have Damien's number, so it was reassuring that I had some helpers on my side. Imani said she would also canvass around the neighborhood and pass out some flyers. I didn't want to waste time, I knew something was wrong, I just didn't know what. After the police left, I went into the office and just began pouring my heart out to God. Asking Him to bring you back, to protect you, and that whoever was responsible, God would deal with them accordingly."

Damien felt his stomach tighten up. It was as though he had a wrench squeezing his intestines. He recalled the intense remorse he felt today, the regret, the pain, not just for Grace, but for everything he had done to other girls, every life he had ruined. *Yo, was it because of Ms. Tasha praying today that I felt so horrible?*" Damien thought.

"Then, maybe about a half-hour later, you came over, Damien. I was a mess. When I saw you, I was excited and suspicious, all at the same time. I thought this guy is either a really good actor, or he really didn't have anything to do with you being missing. I was keeping all of my options open because my daughter was out there somewhere, you know? Anyway, literally five minutes after you left, Bernice knocked on the door. When I looked out the peephole, I almost peed on myself. I'd recognized her.

Grace, remember when I told you about that time your aunt Lina almost got bit by that rattle-snake? I was fifteen, and she was thirteen. We were chillin' at a park we used to frequent when we lived in Arizona. My dad was an Army man, so we moved frequently. Anyway, I was on a bench, and Lina was sitting with your uncles Henry and Simeon at the sand-box nearby."

"The next thing I remember is hearing Lina screaming. I looked up and saw her running toward the boys and this beautiful girl standing there holding this snake. It was still shaking its tail, throwing us warning shots. At that point, I didn't know if they were still warning shots or actual imminent threats. I remember because the noise seemed so loud, and it reminded me of the cicada bugs we used to hear when we lived in Texas. The boys were so afraid, they wouldn't stop crying. I remember thinking to myself, where in the world did this girl come from and how did she just capture that snake, like it was some kind of earthworm. I thanked her so many times for protecting my sister, she even found a pay phone so we could call Animal Control to come get that thing.

"Yep, I said pay phone. This was the eighties; we still had working payphones.

"What's amazing was that Lina was allergic to everything when we were kids, so getting bit by a rattlesnake could've been the absolute worst for her. Someone from the neighborhood nearby was able to get us a box to keep the rattlesnake in until Animal Control got there. I was so grateful that Bernice was there, we got a chance to talk for those twenty minutes it took for them to get there. She was a quiet one, so I was doing a lot of talking, but she was one of the sweetest people I had ever met. I never saw her after that day, but I thought about her from time to time. I looked for her in school, but no one knew who she was.

"Apparently, I never forgot her face, because when she showed up at the door today, I knew exactly who she was. What scared me was that she didn't look a day over fifteen. I'm like, this girl either had what Gary Coleman had, or she's an angel. When I let her in, and she began to fill me in, it was clear. She was indeed, an angel."

Grace and Damien turned to look at one another in awe, completely speechless; all they could do was continue listening.

"First thing she says to me is 'Hi Tasha, I know where Grace is.' Then I let her in, and she spilled all kind of information to me. From Damien's past to his current profession. From the girls in the house to you. From that day in the park to your dad. It was a lot!

"When she first told me about you, Damien, I'm not going to lie, I almost threw up. The mixture of anger and lack of eating was a bad combination. Anyway, she told me the reason she was sent there was to prime my heart to hear what Damien did, and what he really was. She told me that I would have been really harsh, and it could have potentially pushed you further away from Christ. After giving your life to Christ Damien, the last thing you needed was mama bear eating you for dinner. Alive."

"Wait, she knew?" Damien asked. "But how, Grace and I were in the car?"

Grace interrupted. "Damien, well, there's this scripture in the Bible that says 'there's joy in the presence of God's angels when one sinner repents.' Ma, you remember what scripture that is? I can't think of the verse right now."

"No, but I can find out," Tasha replied as she grabbed her phone and searched her Bible app. "Here it is, Luke 15:10."

"Yo, it says that for real?!" Damien asked. Overcome with joy, Damien really didn't know what to say. "How could God still love me so much after everything I've done?" Damien asked, tears welling up in his eyes once more.

Damien, one of the things Bernice told me to tell you is to forgive yourself, and not to keep wondering why and how God could forgive you, but trust that He did and keep moving forward in what He desires for you. God went through all of this to make sure you were good, and He used you to rescue my daughter and those other girls."

"The other girls?" Damien interrupted. "But, I wasn't able to get them out, just Grace."

"No, you didn't get them out, but the police did. Every single one."

"It must have been the call you made, Damien!" Grace excitedly interjected.

"See, it doesn't matter what you were before; you are responsible for making the best out of your second chance. Don't harp on what God already forgave. Make it matter, Damien," Tasha assured Damien.

"So you're not upset for what I did to Grace?" Damien asked Tasha.

"Nah, I'm still upset about what happened to her, I'm a mother. Knowing that my daughter was kidnapped to be sold for sex angers me to my core, but that doesn't mean I haven't forgiven you. Take me, for example. I broke my foot doing Zumba. The pain comes and goes, but the healing process has already started. Just because it's healing, though, doesn't mean it won't hurt me. What you have to make sure to do is not focus so much on what others are going to feel and think. You may encounter a lot of angry parents and loved ones along the way, and it's important that you keep in mind where their frustration is coming from. Be considerate of their grief and pain, pray for them, love them, and for yourself, keep moving. You have to trust God and trust that He has a perfect plan for you. Allow Him to be your strength and your distraction when you feel like you may be headed down to a pit of despair. When people start talking, let them talk. Focus and meditate on God's word and what He says about you. You are not your past; you are not your mistakes, you are not what others say you are, you are who God says you are, period! It's a daily choice Damien, not some magical formula. It's our responsibility to choose Jesus every day, to choose His truth every day, and to avoid temptation every day."

"Whew, I don't think I've cried more in my life than I've cried today," Damien said, forcing a laugh through his tears. Tasha and Grace joined in on the laughter.

"It's good for you; let it out!" Grace exclaimed, tears also falling down her cheeks.

"Also, I think you'd like to know that your friend ... Leon? Is that his name?"

"Yes, ma'am. Is he okay?" Damien asked excitedly.

"Yes, he is going to be okay; the ambulance got him to the hospital in time. He was undergoing surgery to remove the bullet. And the ringleader, well the police caught him up the street from that house, I guess he left Leon bleeding out. He was trying to leave before the cops came, but they got his butt."

"Good," Damien said softly. "I'm next. You know what, though? I'm ready to face the consequences. All the thoughts of what may happen is kinda overwhelming, so I'm ready to deal with it." Wiping the tears from his eyes, Damien put his head down and rubbed it once more.

"Don't worry; you're not alone. First and foremost, you got God, and we will be there for you as well." Tasha reassured him.

"Y'all are?"

"Yeah, goofy, didn't you just hear my mom's whoolllee entire speech, or did you zone out?" Grace responded.

"Nah, I heard it, I just ... that just ... that's not normal. I pretended to be your boyfriend; then I drugged you, then I kidnapped you to be sold for sex. I understand forgiveness and all, but y'all are talking about standing by my side and all that jazz. How could you do that? What does that even look like? I mean, that's unheard of, yo. People in court are going to look at you guys like something is wrong with y'all."

"After all this time, you still think we care about what people think about us, Damien?" Grace responded, putting a reassuring hand on Damien's shoulder. "We're Christians; we're unorthodox. You will get used to it."

Damien couldn't believe the overwhelming amount of love that was being poured out on his behalf. He was floored by the compassion and support he was receiving from two people he had betrayed for months.

"Before we leave for the police station, I wanted to make sure I had this talk with you guys. Damien, it's important that you know you're forgiven, and you're loved and supported. Grace, it's important that you know that despite the unfortunate circumstances, God never left your side. The fact that Bernice was there in all of our lives was just God showing us His love. Sometimes, having that reminder means the world. Damien, she told me that she used to hang around your foster brother. She also told me how amazing he was, and how much he loved God. God's been calling you for a while now, and now that you've finally surrendered, don't look back."

"Ms. Tasha, I'm not one for long speeches, but it doesn't mean I'm not appreciative. I have to say this to both of y'all. From the bottom of my heart, I am sorry. First off, I'm sorry for drugging you last night, Ms. Tasha. That is why you had that headache. Leon and I broke in and used chloroform on you to make sure you stayed sleep. We wanted to be sure you didn't wake up last night and notice Grace wasn't there. It would have ruined our plan." Grace and Tasha shared a quick, expressionless glance then returned their attention to Damien. They already knew what the other was thinking they didn't have to say a word.

"Grace, before I go off to jail for who knows how long, I first have to say I am genuinely sorry. Sorry for putting you through all of that. Sorry for not being the boyfriend you thought I was, the person you thought I was. Sorry for all of the lies and the deceit. Yo, when I first met you at that church event, I was there scouting for girls. But then I got sidetracked when I met you. Since we weren't allowed to be in love and have relationships, I tried to ignore it and treat you like the other girls I recruited. But man, you were different. You were unshakeable. Now looking back, I realize it's because you had God. Those girls that I took advantage of, they were lost and rejected, and I preyed on that. Like a monster. They needed Jesus too. I hope now they get that opportunity. But Grace, your heart, man, don't ever let anyone mess up what's in there. I went there expecting to recruit someone, and I ended up getting recruited. The irony," Damien laughed.

"Bro, you sound like you're on death row heading to the electric chair. Don't sound so end-of-lifey." Grace mocked, forming air quotes. "Nah, on a serious note, I'm going to stay in touch with you. This ain't the end. Despite what you may feel or think, I'm still glad you walked up to my booth that day."

# Chapter 14

The trial was absolutely brutal for the victims. Half of the girls that had been trafficked did not want any part of the trial, they just wanted to move on with their lives, but the other half wanted justice. Justice is what they deserved, and justice is what they got.

Leon was charged with two counts of attempted murder, illegal discharge of a weapon, and human trafficking of minors. He was sentenced to thirty-five years to life in prison.

Rolo was charged with illegal possession of a weapon, utilizing his property for illegal activity, sexual abuse, rape, and human trafficking of minors. He was sentenced to twenty-eight years in prison.

Bella whose real name was Camille, was charged with human trafficking of minors and was sentenced to fifteen years in prison.

Damien was charged with human trafficking of minors and was sentenced to ten years in prison. He received leniency on his sentence for helping officials find the girls and the house.

Grace had given her testimony. She talked about his lies during their entire relationship, how he drugged and kidnapped her, and how he then rescued her. She wanted to make sure that she elaborated on his complete change of heart. During the girls' testimony, they each told the courtroom how Damien was the "nicer" of the three and they were grateful for his help in their rescue. However, they still felt like justice needed to be served for his role.

The prosecutors had witnessed the trauma bond in previous cases, and it was a tough mental fight to have with the victims. They wanted to be their advocates; they didn't want those girls to not receive justice, "even if one of the perps decided to go get a heart from the wizard," as one of the prosecutors said.

Through it all, Damien remained calm and kept his focus on God. He didn't try to fight his own battles; he pled his case, expressed his sincere regret and remorse, sincerely apologized to the victims, and told everyone in the court that he turned himself in and tipped the cops off because he became a Christian. Not just because it was the right thing to do, but he wanted everyone to know Who compelled him.

"I'm a new man now. What I did to those girls was inhuman. This isn't jailhouse religion, or a publicity stunt to get sympathy from you all. I spent my entire life running from the only One who could heal and complete me. This is real. I did what I did to those girls because I was broken myself. It's not an excuse, because I take full responsibility for what I did," Damien said after the lead juror read the guilty verdict. Shortly after, the sentencing was announced. That was like a blow to the chest. Hearing that the next ten years of his life would be spent in prison seemed like the end, but God didn't let him stay discouraged or give him time to soak in self-pity. Immediately after the sentencing was read, he looked over at Grace and saw her mouth the words Keep trusting Him while pointing up. Damien immediately felt a sense of peace. He knew God was with Him, no matter what.

He and Grace stayed in touch; they wrote to each other regularly. Grace never missed his phone calls. Damien insisted on not seeing her until he was free. He didn't want her to visit, because he didn't want to feel the pain of seeing her, then having to say goodbye over and over again. She thought he was being pretty melodramatic in the beginning, but she began to understand his reasoning about a year into his sentence.

At church one Sunday, they had a visitor, Mr. Curtis Chapman, a convicted felon. He was new to the neighborhood and was looking for a new church home. The pastor had connected him with Tasha because he was looking for someone to design a logo for his construction business.

Shortly after, Mr. Chapman became "Curtis" to Tasha, then about a year later, Tasha became Mrs. Tasha Chapman. Grace was so happy for her mom. She hadn't seen her smile that much in years. Curtis was the perfect gentlemen. He wasn't Ernest, and Grace wasn't looking for him to be, but he was perfect for her mom. He was kind, loving, compassionate, patient, and selfless. Not to mention handsome. He was a few months younger than Tasha, so Grace often teased her that she was robbing the cradle.

Thirteen years ago, he was convicted of using his construction business for money laundering and had spent eight years in prison. Curtis had given his life to Christ while in jail, a Christian shared his personal story and helped lead him to the Lord. From that day on, he was never the same. Curtis wanted to make sure he got as close as he could to Christ. He attended church services, had consistent fellowship with the other Christian men, and vigorously stayed in the Word and prayer. He knew that once he got out, he wanted to open another construction business and operate it legitimately this time.

He did just that. He started a new company and named it Chapman's Construction Services. It didn't take long for him to get a steady clientele. He needed to hire more staff because the work did not stop coming. Curtis was aware of who Damien was, and he promised him that he would definitely have a place to work once he was released. During a heart to heart between Grace and Curtis, she complained that Damien didn't want to see her until he got out of prison. Curtis's response to Grace's complaint was, "Grace, he must really like you."

Taken aback by those words, Grace replied, "Like me? Why do you say that? We're friends, that's all."

"Well, to me, it seems like it will hurt him too much to see you, then watch you leave. The more you visit, the more it reminds him that he's stuck in that place."

Surprised by Curtis's explanation, she began to have more compassion for Damien's wishes. She had been angry at him for not allowing her to visit. She felt as though he was shutting her out.

A couple weeks after Grace and Curtis had that discussion, Damien called. He usually called every other day, and they had just spoken the day before, so Grace wasn't expecting his call. As soon as she said hello, Damien began pouring his heart out.

"Grace. Can you hear me?"

"Yes, is everything okay?"

"Yep, just had something to tell you. Did you know that you're one of the best friends I've ever had? Like for real, yo." He elaborated with his east coast accent.

Grace's heart dropped to the pit of her stomach, she loved when Damien let himself be vulnerable. It showed so much progress. "Awe...likewise, Damien!"

That conversation nine years ago began a new chapter in Damien's and Grace's friendship. A fresh start. They used the time Damien was in prison to really get to know each other. No masks, no cover stories, no hidden life, no manipulation, just sincerity.

Damien did what he could to maintain and strengthen his relationship with Christ while he was in prison; he even helped lead a few people to Christ. He also decided it was time to get his GED. So, he took the courses and the test, and passed with flying colors. After obtaining his GED, Damien was motivated to do more. He couldn't stop. He got his AA in human services; then he got a certificate in ministerial counseling. He knew he couldn't undo his past mistakes, but he wanted to make sure he dedicated the rest of his life to serving those who were broken, hurt, abused, mistreated and, he wanted to prevent others from falling into the trafficker life. That was no life to live. That's not even a life.

During Damien's incarceration, Grace stayed busy as well. She went to school and finally decided to attend Southern Orabaul online. She chose the online route to give herself time for her other endeavors. She decided to pursue a degree in human services. Then after obtaining her Bachelor's, she got her Masters, then she topped it off and went on to receive her Ph.D in Biblical Counseling. After her ordeal with sex trafficking, she knew helping victims, especially victims like those at "Hotel Rolo," was her top priority. She knew, without a doubt, that God called her to do that.

She always had a passion for helping people, and it had finally been revealed what she was supposed to do. For the last ten years, Grace was not only going to school but was also building a 501c3 with the help of her friend Imani and her mom.

Grace's ministry would be geared toward providing a safe house for sex trafficking victims and Christian counseling services. Grace saw the impact that the traumatic experience had on those girls, and she wanted to make sure there were resources available to help victims like Latrice, Tamara, Unique Malia, and Brittany. She had even reached out to them and directed them to counseling services in the surrounding areas. Unfortunately, there weren't any close by, which is why Grace was even more pressed to get her vision rolling. People may be more apt to get help when it's right in their face. She'd already secured her board of directors, filled out all the applications, and got her necessary licenses and permits. The last thing she needed was an approved facility, a team of counselors, and a trauma coach experienced with working in a safe house. She also thought about developing a program geared toward former traffickers, it would focus on helping them to change their mindsets, the way they saw people and themselves. It's something she envisioned Damien overseeing.

December 9, 2025, just three days before Grace's twenty-eighth birthday, was the day Damien was being released from prison. Ten years was such a long time. The more Grace thought about that, the more nervous she became. *Why am I nervous?* Grace was baffled. As Grace sat in Curtis's SUV in the prison parking lot, a flood of thoughts began rushing through her head. She couldn't believe she was actually about to see Damien again, after ten long years. The only friend that she'd ever made during a crime, was now one of her best friends. Considering he was the perp, made their friendship ten times weirder. She was excited and nervous; the suspense of waiting to see him was making her crazy. She hadn't seen him in person since the trial. She'd asked Curtis and Tasha to come with her when she picked him up. She didn't know what to expect, and she didn't want it to be weird and awkward, since they hadn't seen one another in ten years.

When Grace caught a glimpse of Damien walking through the gate, she immediately looked in her handheld mirror. *Why did I just do that?* She thought to herself. She checked her teeth, popped a piece of gum in her mouth, and made sure her hair looked presentable. All the nerves she was previously experiencing were gone, just like that. She took her seatbelt off, opened the car door, and walked briskly to meet him. It was about forty degrees outside, and had snowed a couple days earlier, so there were still remnants of snow and ice on the ground. She couldn't walk as fast as she wanted to, because she didn't want to fall on her face. That would be the ideal reunion; they'd never forget that. She laughed out loud as she pictured herself falling on a patch of ice.

When Damien saw Grace, his eyes lit up like a Christmas tree. All his nerves were gone as well. His best friend was there, in the flesh. All he could make out at first was her fluffy green winter coat and brown ankle boots. As she got closer, her face became clearer and it was just as beautiful as he remembered. When Grace finally got to him, their reunion hug was surreal. Damien couldn't believe it was actually real. *I'm actually free. I'm actually walking as a free man. I'm actually hugging my friend, the girl who helped save my life after I almost destroyed hers. God never let me down; He never left my side. Through all the pain, through all of the prison politics, through all of the suicidal urges, spiritual attacks, and loneliness, Jesus never left me. He was there every single day, helping me to forgive myself and keep moving forward, protecting me from falling into temptation, protecting me from giving into suicidal thoughts, and comforting me through the lonely days. And man, was it some lonely days.*

Damien couldn't believe he was out. He constantly battled with allowing God to have mercy on him, because he thought he deserved a much longer sentence for what he'd done. Damien would often say things like, "Once I'm out, I will have served my sentence, but that doesn't change the pain and psychological trauma I caused all of those girls."

It took several years, basically his entire sentence, to allow God to be God. He kept trying to pay for his sins himself. Counseling, praying, and getting in touch with Mr. Chapman all helped him tremendously. Although Mr. Chapman's crime didn't involve trafficking people, some of the money laundered through his businesses was made through drug sales. He hated that he was a part of selling the drugs that people kill each other over. He had also dealt with excessive guilt and trying to pay for his sins himself. Praying, mentoring, and counseling helped him, as well. During Mr. Chapman's visits to Damien over the years, he was able to counsel him and pray with him.

"Man, you don't know how good it is to see you," Grace exclaimed.

"Oh, I can imagine, I look pretty good, huh?" Damien jokingly replied.

"Actually, you do. I was wondering if you were going to look all jail–y, or if you were going to look like twenty years older than you really are, but you ain't changed at all. Why do you still look twenty?"

"Well, you looking pretty twenty-eight–y yourself." Damien joked.

"Twenty-eight–y? What does that look like?" Grace asked, laughing.

"Hmm, I guess sophisticated and doctored up, Ms. Ph.D." Damien replied with a big smile.

"Okay, I guess I look twenty-eight–y then."

Tasha and Curtis were standing outside the car, waiting to greet Damien.

"Oh yeah, I guess they want to say 'hi' to you, too, it is freezing out here," Grace said.

As Damien and Grace walked to the car, Damien could see Tasha's smile from across the parking lot. Over the course of his incarceration, she had become like a mother figure to him. She consistently wrote letters to help keep him encouraged. The closer he got to Tasha and Curtis, the more love he felt. Damien couldn't believe he had these amazing people in his corner.

"Looking good, Damien," Tasha exclaimed as Damien and Grace finally reached the car. Tasha and Curtis took turns giving him a hug.

Good to see you, bro!" Curtis exclaimed.

"Likewise, likewise." Damien responded.

"Damien, you hungry? We were thinking of grabbing some food before heading to the house," Curtis asked.

"Heck yeah, was that a trick question? Man, to eat some non-jail food, yep, I'm hungry."

Everyone laughed.

"Aww, Ma, look at us good Samaritans hanging with these convicted men," Grace joked, drawing laughter from everyone once more.

"Girl, something is wrong with you, let's get out of this cold and go get some food," said Tasha.

# Chapter 15

As they pulled into the plaza parking lot, Grace didn't recognize any of their familiar food spots. It did look familiar; she just didn't know why.

"Y'all found a new restaurant?" Grace asked. No one responded.

"Grace, we wanted to show you something first," Tasha said.

Grace, baffled, looked around, and saw that everyone was smiling. Her stomach began to turn. She loved surprises and hated them all at the same time. They made her feel special and gave her the nerves. Based on the silence and the smiles on everyone's faces, she knew they were up to something, but what? She wondered. *What could they possibly be up to?* She thought of her birthday being a few days away. *Could it be a surprise birthday party?*

As they got out of the car, Damien grabbed her hand so she wouldn't slip on the nearby ice.

"So, remember when I told you I had a friend from church helping me with grant writing?" Tasha asked.

"Yes, I remember."

"Well, a few months ago, it paid off. We'd sent so many proposal packages off, all to no avail. Then finally, we got some good news. We received a grant of $100,000 per year for three years. That will allow us to have the building, the counselor, and three advocates at the safe house twenty-four hours per day. We didn't want to tell you yet because we had this surprise in mind," Tasha explained as she pointed to the top of a very familiar building, where the sign read "Redeeming Grace."

Grace burst into tears. She suddenly knew why the plaza looked familiar. Her dad used to rent space there to teach one of his self-defense classes. She remembered mentioning to her mom that this space would be perfect for what she was trying to accomplish, and it would also allow her to have a piece of her dad in her ministry.

Redeeming Grace was the name God had given her shortly after she was rescued. She knew it was going to be the name of her safe house. She couldn't believe it. She was overcome with so many emotions. She couldn't believe her mom did this.

"We got this done last month, but we wanted to wait until Damien got out," Tasha added.

With tears still pouring from her eyes, Grace was speechless. She walked toward the door.

"Ma, I … I am just speechless right now. I can't believe you did this. This is where I dreamed the safe house would be. I mean, this seems so unbelievable right now. Thank you so much; you are seriously the best. I am so excited! Can we go in?"

"Sure can," Tasha said. "We didn't decorate or anything, we felt it needed to have your touch, and I know that's something you would've wanted to do anyway. You and Imani."

Tasha handed Grace the keys to give her the honor of opening the door to her dream.

"Thanks, Ma." As they walked in, Grace envisioned every victim being helped, healed and set free. She and her staff would care for the victims. They would be reminded daily that there were loved, not forgotten, important, not insignificant, loved, not mistreated, beautiful and valuable, not worthless, and most of all that they were loved by the Savior, Jesus. Redeeming Grace Safe House was not just Grace's dream; it was what she was called to do.

She realized a long time ago that *all things work together for the good to them that love God, to them that are called according to His purpose.* Romans 8:28. She hated what she witnessed at that house that night in October 2015. Those girls and victims alike deserved better, and with the Holy Spirit in her corner; she was going to help give them better ... give them a second chance, give them hope, show them love, speak the truth, teach them about their identity, and provide a safe space for them to heal and be redeemed, by the grace that is only found in Jesus. Redeeming Grace, it began as a rescue mission and ended as rescue mission. This time, it wasn't about her, but about everyone she was called to help.

## Dedication

This book is dedicated to

1.) Every victim of sex trafficking. Jesus sees you. You are beautiful, cherished, and valued!

2.) Everyone who has ever doubted, challenged, or disagreed with the mercy of God.

3.) Every sex trafficker. That person whose life is meaningless to you, Jesus thought they were important enough to die for.

4.) Everyone who has experienced any sort of trauma. Remember "And we know that all things work together for good to them that love God, to them who are the called according to his purpose." Romans 8:28

5.) To every person who has a gift that hasn't been used. Go use it girl. Go use it dude.

5.) To the organizations dedicated to fighting sex trafficking. I applaud you!